Praise for Håkan Nesser

"Nesser has a penetrating eye for the skull beneath the skin."
New York Times

"A deft anatomist of character."
O, The Oprah Magazine

"Nesser is one of the best of the Nordic Noir writers, unafraid of moral ambiguity and excellent at building a brooding atmosphere."
The Guardian

"One of the foremost Swedish crime authors."
The Times

"Håkan Nesser brings a light touch to tales of appalling crime."
Daily Telegraph

"Not all Scandinavian crime fiction is gory and gloomy; it can also be lyrical and delicate, soaked in sunshine and surrounded by beautiful welcoming nature, yet with a touch of suspense gently simmering underneath the idyllic surface. Especially when it's written by Håkan Nesser, one of the Swedish masters of Nordic Noir."
Crime Review

"*The Summer of Kim Novak* is a haunting and evocative novel, beautifully written to draw you into another place and time—a true coming-of-age tale with added mystery."
Liz Loves Books

The Summer of Kim Novak

Håkan Nesser

The Summer of Kim Novak

Translated from the Swedish
by Saskia Vogel

WORLD EDITIONS
New York, London, Amsterdam

Published in the USA in 2020 by World Editions LLC, New York
Published in the UK in 2015 by World Editions Ltd., London

World Editions
New York/London/Amsterdam

Printed by Sheridan, USA

Library of Congress Cataloging in Publication Data is available

ISBN 978-1-64286-019-1

First published as *Kim Novak badade aldrig i Genesarets sjö* by Albert Bonniers
Förlag, Stockholm, Sweden 1998.
Published in the English language by arrangement with Bonnier Rights,
Stockholm, Sweden.

The cost of this translation was defrayed by a subsidy from the Swedish Arts
Council, gratefully acknowledged

Twitter: @WorldEdBooks
Facebook: @WorldEditionsInternationalPublishing
Instagram: @WorldEdBooks
www.worldeditions.org

Book Club Discussion Guides are available on our website.

In memory of Gunnar

I

1

I'm going to tell you about a tragic and terrible event that marked my life—let's call it "the Incident." That fateful event is the reason I remember the summer of 1962 more clearly than any other summer of my youth. It has cast a dark shadow over so much. Me and Edmund. My poor parents, my brother ... that entire chapter of my life. My memories of that town out on the plain—the people, our experiences, and the particulars of our lives—would have been lost to the well of time had it not been for that grisly act. The Incident. But of course, there is more to this story.

Where to begin? I've wrestled with this question, weighed up my options, gone back and forth. Eventually I got tired of following the loose threads of the many possible beginnings and decided to start this story on an average weekday, at home in our kitchen on Idrotts-gatan. Just my father and me, one balmy evening in May 1962. There you have it.

"There are no two ways about it, we're looking at a rough summer," my father said.

He swilled the burnt gravy into the sink and coughed. His back was hunched. He wasn't one for gloom and doom, so I knew that this was serious.

"I'm stuffed," I lied, and rolled the undercooked pota-toes to the meat side of the plate to make it look as though I'd at least eaten half. He came over to the kitchen table and stared at my leftovers. Sadness flickered across his face. There was no hiding things from Dad, but still he took the plate and scraped the remains into the bucket under the sink without comment.

"Like I said, a rough summer," he repeated, his crooked back turned toward me.

"It is what it is," I replied. Those words were his cure-all, and my way of showing him that I wanted to be sup-portive. That we were in this together and that I had in fact picked up a thing or two over the years.

"Truer words were never spoken," he said. "Man pro-poses but God disposes."

"You bet," I replied.

Because it was a mild May evening, I went to Benny's after dinner. Benny was in the bathroom, as usual, so I ended up visiting with his melancholic mom in the kitchen.

"How's your mother?" she asked.

"We're looking at a rough summer," I said.

She nodded and took her handkerchief from her apron pocket and blew her nose. Benny's mom suffered from allergies throughout the summer. They said it was hay fever. Looking back, she seemed to have "hay fever" all year round.

"That's what my dad said," I added.

"There you have it," she said. "Only time will tell."

It was around then that I'd started noticing how adults spoke. It wasn't just my dad. Using this kind of language was a way of showing that you weren't wet behind the ears anymore. Since my mother had gotten so sick she'd landed in hospital, I'd been taking note of the most important expressions and using them accordingly.

It is what it is.

Same old, same old.

It could've been worse.

Life's a mystery.

Or even "Keep your head in the clouds, and your feet on the ground," as Cross-Eyed Karlesson at the corner market remarked a hundred times a day.

Or, as Mrs. Barkman said: "Only time will tell."

Benny was also a Barkman. Benny Jesias Conny Barkman. A guy might think this was a funny set of names, but I never heard him complain.

"We find many names for those we love," his mom would say, with a grin that exposed gums the color of liverwurst.

And then Benny would tell her to "can it."

Even though I had one foot in the adult world, I couldn't help but wonder why people didn't just keep quiet when they had nothing to say. Like Mrs. Barkman—and Cross-Eyed Karlesson. Sometimes when it was busy in the shop, the man didn't stop to breathe when talking to his customers, and truth be told, the sound of it was awful.

When she'd taken the handkerchief from her nose, Mrs. Barkman asked, "How's she doing?"

"Same old, same old," I said, and shrugged. "Not so good, I reckon."

Mrs. Barkman wrung her hands in her lap and her eyes filled with tears, but it was probably just the hay fever. She was a big woman who always wore floral dresses, and my father said she was a touch simple. I had no idea what he meant by that and I didn't really care to find out either. I wanted to talk to Benny, not his weepy-eyed mom.

"He takes a lot of dumps," I said, in an attempt to seem grown-up and to keep the conversation going.

"He has a nervous stomach," she said. "He gets it from his dad."

A nervous stomach? It was the stupidest thing I'd heard that day. Stomachs couldn't be nervous, could they? I chalked it up to her being simple and left it at that.

"Is she still in hospital?"

I nodded. There was no point in talking to her anymore.

"Have you been to visit her?"

I nodded again. Of course I had. What kind of person did she think I was? It had been a week since my last visit, but, you know, it was what it was. The important thing was that my dad was at the hospital almost every day. Even someone like Mrs. Barkman should know this about us.

"You know what they say," she said. "We all have our crosses to bear."

She sighed and blew her nose. The toilet flushed and Benny came running out.

"Hi, Erik," he said. "It's like a horse took a dump in there. Let's get out of here and raise hell."

"Benny," his mum said wanly. "Language."

"Oh crap. Right," said Benny.

Nobody swore as much as Benny did. Not on our street. Not in our school. Probably not even in the whole town. When we were in third grade, or maybe fourth, a finicky teacher with an underbite arrived at school. All the way from Gothenburg. They said she had a natural gift for teaching, and her main subject was Religious

Education. After hearing Benny curse a blue streak for a few days, she decided to sort him out. She was given permission by the headmaster, Mr. Stigman, and our class teacher, Mr. Wermelin, to work on Benny's speech twice a week. I think they started in September and carried on throughout the fall. Around Christmas, Benny developed a stutter so severe no one could understand him. Come spring, the teacher from Gothenburg was fired, Benny started swearing again, and by summer vacation he was back to his old self.

On the May evening my father said we were looking at a rough summer, Benny and I went out to sit inside the cement pipe. At least that's what we did to begin with. The cement pipe was a point of departure for whatever the evening had in store. It lay in a dry ditch fifty meters into the forest, and God knows how it ended up there. It was about one and a half meters in diameter, and just as deep. Because it was tilted on its side, it made a good hideout if you wanted to be left alone. Or needed shelter from the rain. Or were hatching plans and sneaking a few John Silvers that you forced some squirt to buy for you, so you didn't have to show your face at Karlesson's shop, or that you'd bought yourself as a last resort.

On this particular evening we had a couple of cigarettes stashed in a can under a tree-root right beside the pipe. Benny dug them out. We smoked with our usual reverence. Then we debated what sounded better: smokes or weeds. And the right way to hold a cigarette: thumb–index finger or index finger–middle finger. We didn't settle on anything that day either.

Then Benny asked about my mother.

"Your mom," he said. "Christ, is she going to ...?"

I nodded.

"Think so," I said. "Dad says so. The doctors say so."

Benny searched his vocabulary.

"That's some tough luck," he finally said.

I shrugged. Benny had been close to an aunt who had died, so I knew that he knew what he was talking about.

As for me, I had no idea what it was like.

Dead?

When I thought about it—and I'd thought about it often that cold, comfortless spring—all I knew was that it was the strangest word in the whole language.

Dead?

Inconceivable. The worst part was that my dad seemed to have as weak a grip on the concept as I did. I could tell by his face that one time—the only time—I asked what it actually meant. What it actually meant to be dead.

"Hmm, well," he'd muttered, still staring at the TV with the sound turned down. "No one knows, but we'll all find out in time."

"A rough summer," Benny repeated pensively. "For Christ's sake, Erik, you'll have to write to me. I'm going to be up in Malmberget until school starts, but if you need any advice, you can count on me."

There was a lull in our conversation, as if an angel has passed by. I felt it as clearly as anything, and I knew that Benny had felt it, too, because he cleared his throat and solemnly repeated his offer.

"Aw Christ, Erik. Drop me a line and tell me how you're doing."

We shared the last wrinkled cigarette too. I think I did in fact write a letter to Benny; sometime in July maybe, when everything was at its worst, but I can't really recall. What I do know is that I never heard back from him.

He wasn't one for pen and paper, that Benny Barkman. No, sir.

In the early 1960s, my dad worked at the jail. It was a taxing job, especially for someone as sensitive as he was, but he never talked about it, just like he never talked about anything unpleasant.

Sufficient unto the day is the evil thereof, and all that. But still.

He'd arrived in the town on the plain in the 1930s, in the middle of the Depression; met my mother and got her pregnant around the time the world lost its mind for the second time that century. My brother Henry was born on June 1, 1940. Three days later, after taking leave from his post up in Lapland, my father arrived at the bedside of his wife and child, bearing freshly picked lilies of the valley and forty cans of military-issue liverwurst.

So the story goes.

He never went back up north. After his first son was born, he managed to get out of his military service for the rest of the war. He blamed his back, I think. He found a job in one of the town's shoe factories, where the army's winter boots were made. So, in a way, he was still doing his duty. A few years after the end of the Second World War, our family moved into the Idrottsgatan apartment.

As for me, I was born eight years and eight days after my brother, and I grew up with the feeling that our age difference was much greater than the one between him and our parents. However, by the time the early sixties rolled around I'd begun to see that this was somewhat of a misconception. Perhaps my mother's cancer had helped clarify things.

My mother and father were quite old, you see. The summer my mother lay dying, they were both fifty-seven. One hundred and fourteen years in all. A dizzying sum. Henry had turned twenty-two in June. Or was he twenty-three already? I was fourteen. My dad had worked in the prison since the day it opened its doors to the country's most dangerous criminals a year and a half earlier.

Or rather, since it shut its doors behind them.

He was a screw; a word that had never been uttered in the town before the Gray Giant appeared out on the plain.

He called himself a prison guard. Everyone else said screw. A screw at the Gray Giant.

Previously, he'd worked as a shoe-binder at a number of factories. The disappearance of the word "shoe-binder" roughly coincided with the last factory shutting down and the arrival of the screws. So it goes, it seems. Whatever we lose, there's always something there to replace it—events, phenomena, even people. Your head is the only place where everything stays put, but even in there things can go missing.

One factory that didn't shut down during those years was the Jam & Juice where my mother worked. Well, until she got sick, that is. Having a dad at the shoe factory and a mom at the Juicy had its perks: you always had boss shoes and there was usually a stockpile of apple juice down in the cellar.

But we were at the end of an era that summer. There were no perks to having a screw for a dad.

As for my brother Henry, he was expected to continue his studies and then climb up a rung or two on the social ladder, but that didn't really go as planned. He did matriculate at the secondary grammar school—a prestigious all-boys school in Örebro that stood opposite a thousand-year-old castle surrounded by a moat. So far, so good. He busted the books and took the train to the county capital and back every day.

However, just after his second semester, Henry ran away.

It was fall 1957 and it would be more than a year before he knocked on the door at Idrottsgatan again, carrying a sailor bag and a bunch of bananas slung over his shoulder. He'd been around the world, he explained, but had spent most of his time in Hamburg and Rotterdam. He had a rose tattooed on his arm. It was clear to us all that he didn't actually want to move up in the world, at least not in the way our parents had hoped. When Henry returned, my mother cried. I'm not sure if it was out of joy, or in despair over his tattoo. After taking it easy for a few months, Henry set off again, roving the seven seas until 1960. When he came home the next time, on the same day that Dan Waern missed out on the bronze medal for the 1,500 meters in Rome, he said he'd had enough of life on the ocean. He started freelancing for *Kurren*, the regional newspaper, and found himself a fiancée. One Emmy Kaskel, who worked at Blidberg's men's outfitters. She had the best rack in town.

Probably in the whole world.

In just about the same breath he found a studio apartment twenty kilometers away in Örebro, where *Kurren* also had their headquarters. The studio was roughly the size of two ping-pong tables, it didn't have its own toilet or running water, and yet every now and then Emmy Kaskel bared her glorious breasts and more in that shoebox.

At least that's what Benny and I assumed.

But she didn't move in with him. Emmy was two years younger than Henry and still lived with her parents. They were missionaries and had a discount at Blidberg's. My brother said half of our town was involved in the

Free Church choir so it was nothing to worry about.

Whatever they've got, the Free Church has, too, he'd say with a wry smile.

"Well, look who it is," my father said when I came home that mild evening in May.

"Yup," I said. "It's just me."

I could tell something was on his mind, so I sat down at the kitchen table with last year's apple juice and some rusks and flipped through an old issue of *Reader's Digest*, which Grandpa Wille gave us a stack of each year for Christmas. He was the twelfth-best chess player in Sweden and owned a milk bar in Säffle.

"Brace yourself," said my father.

"I'll do my best," I replied.

"You're probably going to have to stay at Gennesaret this summer."

"All right," I said.

"You'll have a good time. I've had a word with Henry. He and Emmy'll be there as well and they'll take care of you."

"I'm sure I'll survive," I said.

"I'm sure you will," said my father. "Edmund might come along."

"Edmund?" I said.

"Why not?" said my father, and scratched his neck. "So you can have some company your own age."

"Well," I said. "It could be worse."

2

The school was three stories tall—shaped like a shoebox and built from yellowish Pomeranian stone that had darkened to brown over the years. On one side of the building was a gravel yard used as a soccer field at recess. On the other side was another playground where you could have played soccer, but no one did.

The anti-soccer crowd kept to this other side, as did the girls, who clustered together, trading things and gossiping. Well, I don't actually know if they traded things, or what they got up to, because I always kept my distance.

I belonged to a group of a dozen or so boys who didn't spend their recess getting dirty on the soccer field. We were the anti-soccer crowd. In my heart of hearts, I hated sports, and I have no idea how all the soccer players fitted on the field each break; there must have been at least fifty of them. But maybe only a score of the best players actually kicked the ball, leaving the others to stand around and shout and make themselves look as though they were in on the action. I don't know. I never watched them play. Like I said, I was on the girls' side. My choice of location wasn't going to impress anyone, but I tried to convince myself that there were more important things in life.

And I wasn't alone. Benny was there, so were Snukke, Balthazar Lindblom, Veikko, Enok, a few others.

And Edmund.

After my father said we might be spending the summer together, I realized I didn't actually know anything about Edmund.

Well, I knew what everyone knew: his father read pin-up magazines, and he was born with six toes on each foot.

Otherwise, he was a blank page. Quite tall and hefty. His glasses always seemed to be missing a lens or a side piece. We'd only been in the same class this past year, and rumor had it he had a whopping model train set and a whopping collection of Wild West magazines, but I didn't know if either rumor was true.

His dad was also a screw; that was the connection. He and my dad had been working together for the past year, and that's probably how they'd started talking about their plans for the summer. One thing must have led to another.

I didn't exactly have any commitments—except maybe with Benny, who was out of the picture the whole summer anyway—so after circling each other warily over the course of a few recesses, I tested the waters.

"Hi, Edmund," I said.

"Hi," said Edmund.

We were standing by the bike racks under the corrugated metal roof, casually kicking gravel at the girls' bikes.

"My dad said something," I said.

"I heard," said Edmund.

"Oh yeah?" I said.

"Yep," said Edmund.

Then the bell rang and that was that for a few days. Not a bad start, I thought.

Gennesaret wasn't the name of the lake. It was the name of a house by a lake called Möckeln. And it's still called that today.

It was twenty-five kilometers from town. It took more than two hours to get there on a bike, but only an hour and a half back. The journey times varied because of Kleva, a punishing hill of over 1,300 meters somewhere around the halfway mark.

There were a number of villages around Lake Möckeln—a large, almost round, brown lake—but mostly it was made up of forest-lined beaches. Gennesaret sat in solitary splendor on a pine-clad headland and was part of my mother's inheritance. A two-floor tumbledown wooden shack with no comforts other than a roof over your head and a fresh-water lake ten meters away. The ice usually took the dock out every winter and there was an outboard motor for the rowing boat that had lain in pieces in the shed since I was born.

My dying mother wasn't the sole owner of this house. There was an Aunt Rigmor who technically co-owned it. However she couldn't be held responsible for her actions and so couldn't claim her share of the inheritance.

Rigmor's tragic condition was the result of an accident that had occurred during one of the first summers of the war. The story had as firm a place in our family history as the Fall does in the Bible: she'd crashed into a moose. What gave the story its mythological shine was the fact that she'd been on a bicycle when it happened. Aunt Rigmor, that is, not the moose. She and a friend had been on a cycling holiday in Småland, and while freewheeling down one of the hills in the uplands she'd charged right into a magnificent twelve-pointer and then straight through the doors of the notorious Dingle asylum on the West Coast.

Never to be discharged, it seemed. I'd only seen pictures of her and she didn't look like Mom in the slightest. She looked more like a seal, actually, but with glasses and no mustache. Fitting for a patient in Dingle.

Who can say if Mom and Dad would have tried to sell Gennesaret, had my tragic aunt not been in the picture, but I think they would have. For some reason, they never seemed to like it out there.

It wasn't cozy. Maybe that was it. Or maybe it was because my mother never learned how to swim. The lake was deep. In parts. Certainly beyond our headland.

Whatever the case, as I went around thinking about it that May I had a hard time picturing how the summer would unfold.

Henry and Emmy, for instance. I couldn't think about Emmy without picturing her breasts—while she was fully dressed, but still—and I couldn't picture her breasts without getting a boner. It was what it was.

And I was hung up on the thought of what my brother would be doing with Emmy Kaskel. Gennesaret wasn't a big house.

And on top of all that, there was Edmund. It was anyone's guess how things would play out.

Whatever, I thought. Only time will tell.

Ewa Kaludis started her job at the Stava School on a Thursday. We'd just had a double period of woodwork and I'd demolished the magazine rack I'd been working on for the past seven months. Our carpentry teacher, Gustav, wasn't happy about it, but it felt pretty good. Whether it was sewing or woodwork, I didn't like arts and crafts; those projects never turned out quite the way you thought they would, and they always took forever.

As usual, I was hanging around the bike shed with Benny and Enok, waiting for recess to end, and then there she was on the street.

I'd like to say I saw her first, but both Benny and Enok are equally sure that they did. Same difference; the point is that she appeared. I realized she must have passed the soccer field first, because within a few seconds the girls' side was overrun with people gawking. Swarms of filthy soccer players.

"Christ," said Benny. He was gawping with his mouth open so wide he might have been waiting for Dr. Slaktarsson, the dentist, to start drilling.

"Would you look at that," said Enok. "It's Kim Novak."

As for me, I said nothing. I wasn't normally one to comment for the sake of it, but at this particular moment I was dumbstruck. It was like in a movie. But better. The birdie who came roaring into the schoolyard on her moped really did look like Kim Novak. Big wheat-blond hair tied back with a foxy red hairband. Dark foxy sunglasses and a full foxy mouth that made me weak at the knees. She wore slim black slacks, a black top that was tight across her chest, and a red-and-black-checked Swanson shirt, open and billowing in the wind.

"Jesus Christ, what a fox," said Balthazar Lindblom.

"A Puch," said Enok. "Holy hell, Kim Novak is rolling into our schoolyard on a Puch. *Kiss me, stupid.*"

With that, Enok fainted. I would have been surprised if he hadn't. He suffered from some sort of mild epilepsy that knocked him out on occasion.

Kim Novak switched off the Puch. She straddled it for a moment with her feet on the gravel, smiling and taking in the 108 figures frozen on the playground. Then she climbed off, elegantly flipped out the kick-stand, took a flat briefcase from the rack, and marched right through the petrified crowd and into the school.

When she was out of sight, I noticed Edmund was standing beside me. Nearly shoulder to shoulder, though he was a bit taller.

When he spoke, his voice was thick with emotion.

"Now that ..." he said, voice thick. "That's what I call a grown woman."

I nodded, thinking of his dad's pin-up mags. I reckoned he knew what he was talking about.

Within two hours, we'd gotten to the bottom of it. The soccer-side of the school had known for a long time that Bertil "Berra" Albertsson was moving to town; we might have known that too if we'd given it some thought. Berra was a handball legend who'd competed in over 150 international matches. It was said that his shots were so hard a goalie would die if they were hit in the head. After twelve seasons in the All-Swedish and national teams, he was going to wind things down by becoming a player-coach for our town's handball team, with the aim of taking it to the top of the league. Even someone like Veikko knew what this meant, and we'd all read about it in *Kurren* a few weeks ago. Super-Berra was going to move into one of the newly built houses over in Ångermanland, and he was taking up his post as Vice President of Parks on the first of July.

What wasn't in the papers was that he was engaged to Kim Novak, and that her name was actually Ewa Kaludis.

Not to mention: she'd be substituting for hopeless old Eleonora Sintring, who'd broken her femur while spring-boarding over a plinth during Housewives' Gymnastics earlier that month.

The day after Ewa Kaludis arrived, several soccer players passed around a sign-up sheet where you could add your name to volunteer to break Sintring's other leg when she came back to work. The idea was that the volunteers would draw straws to see who would do the deed when the time came.

By the time Benny and I wrote our names down, the sheet was already full.

The next Saturday I ran into Edmund in the library.

"Come here often?" I asked.

"Sometimes," said Edmund. "Quite often, actually. I read a lot."

He probably did. I came here once a month at most, so it was no surprise we hadn't run into each other here before.

After all, Edmund was relatively new in town.

"What do you like to read?" I asked.

"Crime," he replied without hesitation. "Stagge and Quentin and Carter Dickson."

I nodded. I hadn't heard of any of them.

"Jules Verne, too," he added after a pause.

"Jules Verne is some pretty choice stuff," I said.

"Choice," Edmund said.

We stood there, not making eye contact.

"So, summer, huh?" he asked.

"What about it?" I said.

"You know, with that place," Edmund said. "Your house."

I couldn't see where he was going with this.

"Huh?" I said.

He removed his glasses and adjusted the tape holding them together. This time he seemed to have broken them at the bridge.

"Christ," he said.

I didn't answer.

After a long silence, he asked: "Can I come or not?"

"'Can I?'" I said. "What do you mean?"

He sighed.

"Well, hell, it's your decision to make," he said.

And then it clicked. I stood there with my tail between my legs and a prickling in my spine.

"Damn straight you can," I said.

Edmund put his glasses on.

"Are you sure?"

"Of course," I said. The prickling stopped.

Then Edmund said: "Cool." He had that thickness in his voice again. "Um ... which trains do you like better: Märklin or Fleischman?"

3

Henry, my brother, was a beanpole. Everyone said so.

He was handsome, too; at least that's what women said. Personally, I didn't have an eye for men's looks at the time, but he did remind me of Ricky Nelson—or rather "Rick" as he had been called since the previous year. I didn't think that was a bad association at all.

Henry smoked Lucky Strikes. He pulled them out of the breast pocket of his white nylon shirt with a gesture that said, "I've been working like a dog, and now it's time to recoup with a smoke."

The year before our mother ended up on her deathbed, he bought his first car—the family's first car, in fact. A black vw Beetle that he drove around in when he was reporting from the countryside. He'd bought a camera, too, so he could take pictures of his accidents and the "victims" of his interviews. I was under the impression that things were moving along pretty well with the freelancing.

Our father used to say so:

"He's getting along well, our Henry."

I didn't really know what "freelance" meant. Henry only seemed to be writing for *Kurren*, but that word was bound up with the others. Lucky Strike. Beat. Freelance.

He'd christened the vw Beetle "Killer."

The following Sunday morning, we were sitting in the kitchen.

"Hey, Erik."

"Yes, Henry?"

Killer was parked out on Idrottsgatan. He'd lit a Lucky and was slurping the dregs of the coffee Dad had made before catching the bus to the hospital.

"We're bunking together this summer."

"So I hear."

He took a drag.

"It's probably for your own good."

I nodded and looked out of the window. The sun was shining brightly. On a day like this, you could swim in Lake Möckeln.

"Mom's situation isn't too good," said Henry.

"Yup," I said.

With his elbows on the table, he looked out at the sunshine.

"Nice weather."

I nodded.

"We could take a spin and check the place out. Gennesaret, I mean."

"Sure," I said.

"Are you game?"

"I've got nothing else to do," I said.

Henry and I did some sorting out in Gennesaret that Sunday.

We tidied up and prepped for the summer. We dragged all the mattresses and pillows and blankets on to the lawn so the sun could draw out the winter's damp. We aired out the house and swept the floors. Upstairs and down. There wasn't really that much to do. On the ground floor there were two rooms and a small kitchen with a basin that drained into a dry well, a refrigerator and a stove. To get to the top floor you walked up a stairway on the gable wall. Two rooms in a row. A slanted roof. When the sun was out, it was scorching up there.

We had a swim. We found the dock in its usual spot among the reeds at the southern end of the point. Henry said he'd turn it into a floating pontoon dock this year. I nodded and said that it was a boss idea.

"But we'll need better planks," Henry said.

We sunbathed on the mattresses and chatted. Well, actually, we smoked. Henry gave me two Luckys and swore he'd wallop me if I told Dad.

I wasn't planning on saying anything anyway. We drove home in the middle of the afternoon, during the hottest part of the day. Henry had a soccer game to watch that night. We brought both propane tanks with us, the one for the stove and the one for the refrigerator, so we could get them refilled in time for the summer.

It wasn't a bad Sunday at all, and I thought the summer might even be bearable.

Difficult, but bearable.

I was more interested in Edmund's dad's magazines than I was in Edmund's Fleischmann, but I kept that to myself.

Edmund's room was around eight square meters in size and the fiberboard holding the model railway took up about six of them. All in all it was well organized. He slept on a mattress under the board, where he also had a lamp, a bookshelf, and a few drawers of clothes. I didn't see any Wild West magazines.

"Should we rebuild it?" said Edmund.

"Okay," I said.

We rearranged the whole landscape in two hours, drove the train around, and orchestrated some nifty crashes before we got bored.

"Building it up is actually the best part," said Edmund. "After that, it just sits there."

"Agreed," I said.

"One of my cousins gave me all this," Edmund said. "He got married and his wife wouldn't let him keep it."

"Well," I said. "That's how the cookie crumbles."

"You have to choose your woman wisely," Edmund said. "Let's grab a Pommac from the kitchen."

We grabbed a Pommac in Edmund's kitchen and I wanted to ask him about the pin-up mags and about him having twelve toes instead of ten, but I never quite found the right moment.

Instead, we cycled home to Idrottsgatan and had an old apple juice. I took Edmund into the woods, too, and showed him the cement pipe. He thought it was choice— at least, that's what he said. Then he realized he should have been home for dinner half an hour ago, and we each went our separate ways.

Stava School's staffroom was on the girls' end of the third floor. It featured a sizable balcony, the only one on the building, and as summer vacation approached the teachers would sit up there under colorful parasols, drinking coffee and smoking. We never actually saw them from the playground, but we heard them arguing and laughing and we could see their clouds of smoke.

During Ewa Kaludis's brief sojourn at the school, the balcony routine changed quite a bit. People had started to stand while smoking instead of just sitting. They leaned over the railing and gazed out over the play-ground. She was the one who started doing that, and of course the studs crowded around her, puffing away and grinning.

Stensjöö, the deputy head teacher. Håkansson the Horse. Brylle.

"Check out Brylle, fer Christ sake," said Benny. "He's giving it to her from behind."

"Fat chance," said Balthazar Lindblom. "No way he'd dare. You can look but you can't touch, right? If they so much as laid a finger on her, Super-Berra would come down here and beat them up."

"No question," said Veikko. "He'd knock their heads right off with one throw of his ball. What a guy."

The girls' side was unusually crowded during those days in late May. Quite a few soccer players seemed to have developed nobler interests, and the bike shed was packed. Ewa Kaludis only taught our class and one other, so most kids had to grab any opportunity they could to gawk at her.

Like during breaks when she was up on the balcony. Kim Novak. Ewa Kaludis. Super-Berra's super-girl.

I was one of the lucky ones. We'd had Sintring in English and Geography before she stumbled over the pommel horse. Håkansson had jumped in and subbed for a few weeks, but now we'd been hit with Ewa Kaludis. With only three weeks to go until summer vacation. It was torture.

She didn't have to teach us. There was no need. We were plugging away. Whenever she entered the class-room, we sat in rapt silence. She would smile and her eyes sparkled. It gave us all the chills. Then she would sit down on the teacher's desk, cross one leg over the other, and tell us to keep working on one page or another. Her voice reminded me of a purring cat.

We worked diligently. Ewa Kaludis either sat on her

desk, sparkling, or walked around swiveling her hips as she moved between the desks. If you raised your hand, she'd almost always stand behind you, a little off to the side. When she leaned forward, her breasts would rest against your shoulder. Or, rather, one of her breasts would. Only the boys seemed to need any help, and the air in the classroom was heavy with her perfume and with restrained young desire.

I didn't really know what the girls thought of Ewa Kaludis, because the girls and I never shared our experiences, but I reckoned that they benefited from her presence as well. In their own female way. I could be wrong. Maybe they were all jealous as hell.

Once when I raised my hand and she came over to help, I almost fainted when her breast brushed against my shoulder and cheek. I remember thinking: if this is my time to go, then so be it.

She noticed, I think, because she put her hand on my arm and asked me how I was. Of course, that only made it worse, but then I bit down on my tongue, which helped straighten me out.

"I'm not feeling very well," I said. "I think I'm getting my period."

I have no idea why I said that, and Ewa Kaludis just laughed. Benny, who was sitting next to me and was the only other person who heard that gem, said he'd never heard any damn thing like it.

"Aw hell, Erik. You'll be sitting pretty after that. No doubt about it."

Maybe he was right. Who knows? Mostly I was just relieved that she didn't get angry.

"Let's wait a sec," my father said. "They're not done with their rounds yet."

I nodded, hugging the bag filled with grapes from the Pressbyrån kiosk, wrinkling it even more.

"Don't crush the grapes," my father said.

"I won't," I said.

We sat in silence on the green benches. Nurses whizzed by, smiling kindly at us.

"The rounds always take time," said my father. "They've got lots to do."

"I know."

"Why don't you go comb your hair. You have time. There's a bathroom over in the corner."

I went and combed my hair with my new steel comb. I had broken off five of the teeth from the slim end so I could pick the locks on the toilets at the train station. It didn't work, but that was beside the point. The important thing was that those teeth were missing. If you were someone who kept to the girls-side and didn't have a steel comb, you were worth less than a burst bicycle tube. It was what it was.

"It's almost time," said my father when I came back out.

"I know," I said. "But there's no rush."

"You bet," said my father.

She tried to hug me, but I stroked her arm instead, which was just as good. My father sat to her right, and I to her left.

"We brought grapes," said my father.

"Lovely," said my mother.

I put the Pressbyrån bag on top of the yellow hospital blanket.

"How's school?" my mother asked.

"Good," I said.

"You're taking the day off?"

"Yes."

She peered into the bag, then closed it.

"And how are things at home?"

"No problems there," I said. "Dad burns the gravy sometimes, but he's getting better every day."

My mother smiled, shutting her eyes as though it was taking a lot out of her. I looked at her. Her face was grayish-blue and her hair looked like wan grass.

"No problems at all," I said. "Is there a bathroom here?"

"Of course," my mother said, her voice weak. "It's out in the corridor."

I nodded and left. I tried to take a dump for twenty-five minutes, and then I went back in.

My mother and father were sitting very close to each other, whispering. They fell silent when they noticed me. I took my seat on her left.

"Are you going to Gennesaret soon?" my mother asked.

"Yes, we are," I said. "Henry and I have been there already to put some things in order."

"I'm glad Emmy and Henry are taking care of you."

"Yes," I said.

"Henry's getting along well," my father said.

There was a pause.

"It was nice of you to visit," my mother said.

"It was nothing," I said.

"I think we'll get going now," my father said. "So we can catch the quarter-past bus."

"You do that," said my mother. "I'm all taken care of here."

"I'll stop by tomorrow after work," my father said.

"No need," said my mother.

I got up and patted her on the arm and then we left.

I took out my Colonel Darkin books and counted them. Yes, right. Six of them. Six black waxed-paper notebooks with forty-eight pages in each. Five of the notebooks were full; the sixth had almost been brought home.

I stuffed Darkin's completed adventures back into the plastic bag and pushed them to the back of my underwear drawer. It wasn't an ideal hiding place; I'd often thought of finding someplace better—maybe I could bury them in a bag out in the forest. Further along in the dried-out ditch: they'd be safe and sound out there.

But I hadn't got around to it. Of course, the underwear drawer was much safer now that my mother was in hospital. My father wasn't the one who rooted around in my things. He barely ever came into my room at all.

I'd created Colonel Darkin about two years earlier. I'd been given one of those notebooks as a birthday present by Linda-Britt, my fat, buck-toothed cousin who thought I should keep a diary because she kept one herself and found it very enriching.

There weren't even any lines in the notebook, which was strange considering that she wanted me to write in it. So I used a ruler and divided each page up like a comic book, four panels per side, only on the right-hand pages, forty-eight parts; and with that I was on my way with *Colonel Darkin and the Golden Gang*. It was an adventure story set between London, Askersund, and the Wild West, and it had everything you could ask for: double-crossing, incorruptible honor, and razor-sharp lines.

"You have exactly one second to answer me, Mr. Frege, my time is valuable."

"That's a mighty fine body you have there, Miss Carlson. Are you planning on keeping it?"

"Sweet moose antlers, Nessie, you forgot to spike the tea with rum."

Colonel Darkin himself was a battle-scarred sleuth who'd retreated to his log cabin in the mountains, and only poked his head out when the world needed him. He had his busty blonde niece for a sidekick, who wielded power over the opposite sex. I named her Vera Lane, and it was love at first panel.

At the moment, she was locked away in an attic tower belonging to a mad scientist called Finckelberg. He had just roared off into town in his Ferrari to buy gasoline so he could burn her up. Darkin was a hundred kilometers away, speeding towards her on his motorcycle, a BSA 300 LT with diamond spokes. I had to make sure he reached her before the flames began to lap at her lovely body; but I only had eight pages left in the notebook, and I was terrible at drawing fire.

I was no great comic-book artist, even I knew that. But I did feel a certain responsibility toward the characters I'd created. If I didn't write about them and keep drawing them, they'd just sit there in the underwear drawer like abandoned marionettes.

Sometimes it felt like a chore. But for the most part—especially when I was on a roll—it was one of the most meaningful things I did during my childhood. Maybe it felt that way because those were the only times I managed to leave the troubled world behind.

I'd never shown them to another living soul. And I'd never told anyone about Colonel Darkin.

It was that kind of hobby.

I opened an apple juice, took two large gulps. I thought for a while.

"Goddammit!" I wrote in Colonel Darkin's speech bubble. "I should've known there'd be a catch."

4

Henry, my brother, wrote about everything for *Kurren*.

City-council meetings, speedway contests, and suspected arson. Two-headed calves and siblings meeting for the first time after fifty-seven years. What he didn't fish up from the news desk or from the local area, he found in other newspapers, both Swedish and international. He spent at least an hour a day in the Örebro library skimming the news and sensational headlines from all over the world, looking for leads for his own stories.

He cut out everything he'd written that had made it to print and glued the clippings into large scrapbooks. By this point in the summer, he already had half a dozen scrapbooks, which he'd let me leaf through when I visited his shoebox on Grevgatan. I liked curling up in his sagging bed, which had iron bars on the head- and footboards, and perusing the headlines. I rarely read the articles, but the headlines spoke to me; at that time I didn't know that it was usually someone other than Henry who came up with these beauties: "Sly Sow Stows Away for Seventy km Ride"; "Schnapps: Good for Your Blood Pressure"; "German Ministers on French Leave in Arboga."

After I read a headline as good as that, I'd close my eyes and try to picture the complicated reality hidden behind it.

Sometimes I could, sometimes not.

"Just one thing," Henry said, one day when there was less than a week left of spring semester.

I looked up from a clip about a fireman from Flen who had fractured both femurs in Frövi.

"Yeah?" I said.

Henry studied his cigarette and then put it out in the wet sand inside the monkey's skull that he kept next to his Facit Privat typewriter.

"About the summer."

He's backing out, I thought. For Christ's sake.

"What about it?" I said.

"A couple of things," he said and looked more like Ricky Nelson than ever. Or Rick, rather. I closed the scrapbook.

"I'm taking time off from *Kurren*."

"Uhuh."

"The whole summer."

"The whole summer?"

"That's right. I'm going to write a book."

It was like he was talking about going down to Karlesson's to buy a popsicle.

"A book?" I said.

"Yup. It has to happen sometime."

"Oh yeah?"

"Some people have to. I'm one of those people."

I nodded. I was sure he was. I didn't really know what to say.

"What's it going to be about?"

He didn't answer right away. He put his feet up on his

desk, took a gulp of Rio Club from the bottle on the floor, and fished out a fresh Lucky Strike.

"Life," he said. "The real deal. Existentially speaking."

"Uhuh," I said.

He lit his cigarette and we sat there. Henry took a few deep drags, his shoulder blades hooked on the back of the chair. He stared up at the ceiling where the smoke was dissipating.

"Good," I said finally. "It's cool that you're writing a book. I bet it'll really be something."

He didn't seem to care what I had to say.

"Was there anything else?" I asked.

"Like what?" said Henry.

"You said there were a couple of things. The book, that's just one, right?"

"You've got one heckuva head for numbers, brother," said Henry. "A real-life calculator."

"At least when it comes to counting to two," I said.

Henry laughed. He had a curt, sharp laugh. It sounded cool and I tried to copy it, but it didn't really work. It was hard to learn how to laugh like someone else.

"Well, it's about Emmy," said Henry, and then he blew a ring of smoke that soared through the room like a sputnik.

"Out of sight," I said when it hit the wall and vanished. "What about Emmy?"

"She's not coming," said Henry.

"What?" I said.

"She's not coming to Gennesaret."

"Why not?"

"I dumped her," said Henry.

I wasn't sure what that meant. Unless he meant that he had beaten her to death and thrown her into a canal with her feet stuck in cement blocks, and that didn't seem likely. Vera Lane had been close to getting that treatment in *Darkin III*, but I couldn't imagine Henry doing something like that.

"Cool," I said, trying to sound neutral.

"So it's just going to be you and me and your pal. What's his name?"

"Edmund," I said.

"Edmund?" said Henry. "Christ, what a name."

"He's okay," I said.

"Sure, sure," said Henry. "You can't judge a person by their name. I slipped it to a skirt called Frida Assel once. In Amsterdam. She wasn't bad, not bad at all."

I nodded and sat there thinking about all the skirts with strange names that I'd slipped it to.

And all the skirts I'd dumped.

"Let's keep Mom and Dad in the dark," Henry said.

"What do you mean?"

"About Emmy not being there. They'll just worry that we won't be able to feed ourselves and all that," my brother Henry said. "But we will. Three guys in their prime."

"You bet," I said. "No problem. I'm a wiz with omelettes."

And then Henry laughed his sharp laugh. It felt good. It occurred to me that when my brother laughed, it was like having your head scratched.

One day during the last week of school we went on a field trip to Brumberga Wildlife Park. I stuck with Edmund, Benny, and Enok the whole time, and even though an all-girls' team beat us at the quiz by one lousy point and we lost out on the tub of ice cream, the afternoon wasn't half bad. Enok had just celebrated his birthday and raked in a whole fifty-kronor note from his slow-in-the-head uncle, so we were rolling in it. Enok wasn't one to hold back. He wolfed down fifty-four Dixi caramels and had to sit in one of the sick-seats on the ride home.

I ate thirty-six Reval sweets myself and felt fantastic.

The next night I had a dream. I was at the wildlife park again and the whole class was standing in front of a large green aquarium with dolphins, rays, and seals. Sharks, too, I think. We were all still and quiet because Ewa Kaludis was speaking. Behind her, the large torpedo-like bodies continued their eternal journey round and round in the green water.

Then I heard Benny swear. He lifted his dirty index finger and pointed and I saw at once what he'd discovered.

My mother was floating by in the aquarium.

Among the rays and seals. My mother.

It made me feel awful. She was wearing her threadbare blue house dress, the one with the faded roses, and she looked swollen and bug-eyed. I rushed over to the glass, waving at her to move to the other side, but she just hung there in the water and stared at us with her sad eyes. It seemed impossible to get her to move, so I turned around. Pressed myself against the glass and spread out my arms, trying to hide her. Ewa Kaludis stopped speaking and gave me a curious look. She seemed disappointed, and I wanted to cry and wet myself and be swallowed up by the earth.

When I woke up it was quarter to five in the morning and I was soaked through with a cold sweat. I thought it had to have something to do with the Reval caramels. I got out of bed and sat on the toilet to no avail.

As I sat there I thought about the dream. It was weird. Brumberga Wildlife Park didn't have an aquarium, and Ewa Kaludis hadn't even been on the trip with us.

I couldn't get back to sleep that night.

Just before I walked into the apartment, Edmund said:

"What's the biggest difference between two things in the world?"

"The universe and Åsa Lenner's brain?" I said.

"Nope," said Edmund. "It's between my dad and my mom. Just so you know."

I found out he wasn't wrong over the dinner they'd invited me to, which I think was meant to be an advance thank you for letting Edmund stay at Gennesaret all summer.

Albin Wester, Edmund's father, was short and stocky, with limp arms and a rolling gait. He looked like a silverback; a bit worn-out and resigned too. Even though I was anti-soccer, I was reminded of a soccer coach trying to come up with a play during half-time when the team was down 6–0. Upbeat, but somehow unwell. He talked throughout the meal, especially when his mouth was full.

Mrs. Wester looked as severe as a Mora clock draped in a mourning shroud. She didn't say a word during dinner, but tried to smile every so often. And when she did, she seemed on the verge of cracking, and then she'd hiccup and squeeze her eyes shut.

"Dig in, boys," said Albin Wester. "You never know when you'll get your next meal. Signe's sausage hotdish is famous across northern Europe."

Both Edmund and I ate plenty, because it was a very good hotdish. I thought of the domestic situation facing us that summer and told Edmund to ask his mom for the recipe.

I knew that kind of thing was considered the height of good manners, and as if on cue the Mora clock cracked open and hiccupped.

"Sausage Hotdish à la Signe," said Albin Wester out of

the corner of his mouth. "Food fit for the gods."

He smiled, too, and a few pieces of sausage fell in his lap.

"She's an alcoholic," Edmund explained afterward. "She has to tense every muscle in her body to get through a dinner like this."

I thought that sounded strange and said so. Edmund shrugged.

"Eh," he said. "It's not strange at all. She has three sisters. They're all the same. They take after their dad—that man drank like a fish—but the female body can't seem to take it."

"Really?" I said.

"You shouldn't give womenfolk schnapps. Or put gunpowder in their tobacco. It's too much for them."

"You sound like Salasso," I said. "Do you read lots of Wild West magazines?"

"Sometimes," said Edmund. "But lately I prefer books."

"I like to mix it up," I said diplomatically. "How long has she been like that, by the way? Can't you cure her a little?"

I wasn't entirely unfamiliar with the ills of alcohol. My father's cousin Holger was cut from the same cloth and in fourth grade we'd had a teacher for half a semester who went by the name Finkel-Jesus. He'd sneak drinks from his desk drawer throughout the school day and was fired after he fell asleep in the staffroom and wet himself.

Or so rumor had it.

Edmund shook his head.

"We keep it in the family," he said. "It's not officious."

"Uh-huh," I said. "But I think the word is 'official.'"

"Who cares what it's called," said Edmund. "Either

way, she's why we move so often. At least, I think so."

And then I felt sorry for Edmund Wester.

And for his dad.

And maybe I felt a little sorry for Mrs. Wester, too.

We went to see a Jerry Lewis film at the Saga that evening. That was also the Westers' treat.

"Christ," Edmund said while we walked home. "Everyone should be like Jerry Lewis. Then the world would be boss."

"If everyone was like Jerry Lewis," I said, "then the world would have gone under thousands of years ago."

"Clever," he said. "We do need Perry Mason types too; you're absolutely right."

"Paul Drake and Della," I said.

"Paul Drake is really something," said Edmund. "The way he walks into the courtroom in the middle of a cross-examination and winks at Perry. That's one heckuva guy!"

"And he always wears a white blazer and black trousers," I said. "Or maybe it's the other way around."

"Always," said Edmund.

"Della is in love with him," I said.

"Objection," said Edmund. "Della is in love with Perry."

"The hell she is," I said. "She's in love with Paul Drake."

"Okay," said Edmund. "She's in love with both of them. No wonder."

"That's why she can't choose between them," I said. "Objection sustained."

We went around spouting one-liners for a while.

"Objection overruled."

"Objection sustained."

"Your cross-examination."

"No further questions, your honor."

"Not guilty!"

Edmund lived further up on Mossbanegatan and I lived down by the sports center, so we parted at Karlesson's shop. Karlesson's had just closed for the evening; its green windows were shut and the chewing-gum dispenser was chained to the bike rack and locked with a padlock.

"Did you know you can use broken sausage forks in the gum dispenser?" I asked Edmund.

"What?" said Edmund. "What do you mean?"

I explained. All you had to do was break off a centimeter of the end of the flat wooden spoons they give out with mashed potato. Ice cream spoons worked too, but they were harder to find. Then you pushed the wooden bit into the twenty-five-öre slot and gave it a turn. No problem. Clickety click. Shake shake. Worked every time.

"You're kidding," said Edmund. "Are you game?"

We dug around in the trash can mounted to the wall and finally found a sticky ice-cream spoon. I measured and broke it off against my thumbnail. We waited for a gang of giggling girls to pass by, and then we did the deed.

Four balls and one ring.

We each took two balls and Edmund took the ring to give to his alcoholic mother.

"Slick," said Edmund. "We should come here one night this summer and clean it out."

I nodded. I'd been plotting to do just that for a long time.

"All you need are the spoons," I said. "But there are always some on the ground near the hot-dog stands. Herman's and Törner's on the square."

"One of these nights, we'll do it," said Edmund.

"Sustained," I said. "One night this summer."

Then we said our see-you-laters and went our separate ways.

I knew my brother Henry was an unusual person, but I didn't know just how unusual until that comment he made one evening; it must have also been during the last week of school.

"Super-Berra is an asshole," he said.

I was the one who'd brought him up. Or rather, I'd brought up Ewa Kaludis, probably something about her being with Berra.

"Like I said, a real asshole."

It was a simple statement; it caught me by surprise, so I didn't know how to respond and we changed the subject and then Henry left for a Maranatha meeting in Killer.

After he'd gone, I wondered why he'd even say something like that, and then I remembered that he'd interviewed Bertil Albertsson once for *Kurren*, when he'd moved to town in early May.

Super-Berra: an asshole?

I wrote it on a piece of paper and stuck it in *Colonel Darkin and the Golden Lamb*. The statement had been so remarkable I'd wanted to preserve it somehow.

Later in the summer I'd have a reason to think more deeply about this. A big reason. But I didn't know that then, and the scrap of paper must have disappeared somehow, because I never saw it again.

5

This year was our last real graduation ceremony of primary school.

Some of the class would go on to eighth grade; about half of us would transfer to KCJSS, the Kumla County Junior Secondary School, in the fall. Those of us who hadn't already quit after sixth grade, that is. It was a waypoint; among other things I would never again sit in the same classroom as Veikko and Sluggo and Gunborg and Balthazar Lindblom.

It didn't really matter, but I'd miss a few of them. Benny and Marie-Louise, for instance. Well, Benny I'd see in the cement pipe and around town, but I'd never again be able to sit and fantasize about Marie-Louise and her lovely dark curls and her brown eyes. At least not at close range.

But I'd get over it. I'd never really made any progress with Marie-Louise anyway. I was sure there would be other foxy skirts in the secondary school. And if you missed your chance with one, there'd be a thousand more to take her place. *C'est la vie.*

But how would I live without Ewa Kaludis? This question suddenly—and unhappily—opened up like an abyss. It was as if her breast had stayed pressed against my shoulder since I told her that I was getting my period. Ewa visited our classroom on graduation day just as Brylle was opening the present that the girls had bought him: a large framed picture of a gloomy moose standing at the edge of a forest. Everyone knew that Brylle hunted moose for a week every autumn, and now he was standing there behind his desk staring at the picture, forcing a wide smile.

"I just want to thank you all for the time we shared," said Ewa Kaludis. "It has been a pleasure teaching you. I hope you have a good summer break."

By light years, it was the most spiritual thing I'd heard in my fourteen-year-old life. Her hips swayed as she left the room, and an ice-cold hand gripped my heart.

Damn it, I thought. Is this how she's going to leave me?

The moment was paralyzing. There at my desk, I learned what it was like to lose something invaluable. How it must feel in the seconds before you throw yourself in front of a train.

As luck would have it, no train rolled through the classroom.

"What's with you?" said Benny when we were basking in the sunshine on the playground. "You look punch-drunk. Like Henry Cooper in the twelfth round."

"Oh," I said. "It's just my stomach. When are you leaving?"

"In two hours," said Benny. "I'll get there tomorrow morning. It's a long damn way to Malmberget. I hope it works out for your mom."

"I'm sure it will," I said.

"I'm going down to Blidberg's to buy a Bonanza shirt," Benny said. "And one of those red bloody ties—I've got to impress the cousins. See you in the fall."

"Say hi to those damn Lapps and the mosquitoes for me," I said.

"You bet," said Benny. "Write to me if it turns out to be a rough summer."

My brother Henry had already installed himself at Gennesaret. As far as my father knew, Emmy Kaskel was with him, but of course I knew better. The idea was that Edmund and I would cycle the twenty-five kilometers there on Sunday and join them. Henry could've given us a ride, of course, but leaving our bikes behind was out of the question. There were plenty of interesting places to explore in the forests around Lake Möckeln. Without our bikes, we'd be like cowboys without their trusty steeds; that's what Edmund and I thought.

On the Saturday night my father and I visited the hospital again, me in my graduation outfit, Dad in a blazer, shirt, and tie. He never wore a tie at work or around the house, but when he went to the hospital, he dressed up. Even though he took the bus almost every day. I wondered why, but I didn't want to ask. Not on that day either.

My mother was in the same bed in the same room and seemed mostly unchanged. Her hair was newly washed and looked a little nicer. Like a sort of halo on her pillow.

We'd brought a bag of fresh grapes and a bar of chocolate, but after an hour with her, as we were leaving, she gave me back the chocolate.

"Take it, Erik," she said. "You need some meat on those bones."

I didn't want it, but I took it anyway.

"I hope you have a good time at Gennesaret," my mother said.

"You bet I will," I said. "Take care."

"Send my regards to Henry and Emmy," she said.

"I will," I said.

On the bus home, my dad talked a lot about what we could and couldn't do at Gennesaret. What we should keep in mind and what we absolutely could not forget. The propane and what not. He was trying to hide the note he had in his hand, which my mother must have given him while I was in the bathroom. I could tell by his tone that he didn't really care about the advice he was giving. He trusted Henry and Emmy. He rambled on out of duty and empathy with Mom. I felt sorry for him.

I really do believe he trusted me, too.

"I might stop by some time," he said. "And you'll come to town every now and then, won't you?"

I nodded, knowing that this was mostly just talk. Things you say to make yourself feel better.

"But I'm working three more weeks. And I'll want to visit her at the weekends."

It was strange that he said "her" instead of "Ellen" or "your mother," as he usually did.

"It is what it is," I said. "We'll be fine."

I took out the chocolate bar—a Tarragona—the one that had been for my mother, but that she'd given back to me. I handed it to my dad.

"Do you want some?" I said.

He shook his head.

"You take it. I'm not in the mood."

I put it back in the inner pocket of my jacket. We passed through Mosås, past the peat-moss bog where Henry had worked for a couple of summers before he went to sea; I tried to picture Ewa Kaludis's face, but I wasn't having much luck.

"If you find the time, tar the boat," my father said when we turned into town at the junction. "It couldn't hurt."

"Will do," I said.

"The dock isn't up to much, I suppose."

"We'll take care of that too."

"Only if you have the time," my father said and hid the paper my mother had given him. "The rest is up to you."

"Who knows what the future holds," I said.

"Keep your head in the clouds and your feet on the ground," said my father.

When we got off the bus at Mossbanegatan, I dropped the Tarragona in the trash can mounted on the bus stop post.

I regretted it all the way home to Idrottsgatan, but I didn't go back to get it.

A man's gotta do what a man's gotta do, I thought.

The weather was changeable, sun and clouds, on the Sunday as Edmund and I left town. And there was gentle headwind. As we pedaled through Hallsberg it started to rain and so we went into Lampa's bakery outside the station and each had a Pommac and a cinnamon bun. Edmund tossed a krona into the jukebox. Drinking our Pommacs and staring out at the rain, we listened to "Cotton Fields" three times in a row. There were no other tunes in the jukebox worth spinning, Edmund said, and I took him at his word.

And "Cotton Fields" was one heckuva song.

I had warned Edmund about the Kleva hill, but that had only pumped him up to perform a grand feat on this, our first day of summer vacation.

"I'm going to do it all in one," he said. "I'll put fifty öre on it."

"I'll give you one krona," I said because I knew the stakes. "You can't do all of Kleva without a racing bike."

Both Edmund and I had second-hand bicycles without

any customizations other than baskets and bells. No banana seats. No gears. No brakes on the handlebars. At least Edmund's was a Crescent. Mine was a pale green Ferm, and it was nothing to write home about.

"I'm going to give it my best shot," declared Edmund as the hill came into view. "No further questions."

He made it almost halfway up. And then we had to sit on the roadside for fifteen minutes until Edmund's legs would start obeying him again. His face was pale when I came up to him and a light froth had formed at the corners of his mouth. He lay on his back at the edge of the ditch, legs shaking, his bike beside him.

"That's one hell of a hill," he groaned. "In Sveg where we used to live there was a real killer, but this one was much worse, I tell you. Careful, I was a little bit sick over there, don't sit in it."

He pointed and I lay down at a safe distance. I clasped my hands behind my neck and squinted up at the clouds crowding together and thinning out as they moved across the sky. Edmund was still breathing heavily and seemed to be having trouble speaking, so we lay like this for a while, just *being there*.

Being there on the roadside halfway up the Kleva hill. One Sunday in June 1962.

This would have been out of the question had this been Benny instead of Edmund; it would've been impossible to simply lie still. We would've been smoking and swearing up a storm, but with Edmund I could just be silent without it feeling strange at all.

Not this time—when he was about to faint from lactic acidosis—and not the next times either. Talking was optional; it was that simple. I couldn't put my finger on why. Was it because his mother was an alcoholic or because they'd lived up in Norrland for so long? It didn't matter. The point was that it could be this way; Edmund's silence was a good thing and I decided to tell him this after I got to know him a little better.

In a few days or so.

Henry had snapped up more than sixteen cans of Ulla-Bella's meatballs in brown gravy for a song at Laxman's—the convenience store in Åsbro, a village that lay a few kilometers away from Gennesaret—and on that first night we ate two of them.

As well as potatoes with the skin on and lingonberries Henry had brought with him from town. We had a choice of milk or apple juice.

It tasted decent. Edmund and I did the washing up while Henry sat outside on one of the deck chairs with his coffee and cigarettes. Occasionally he wrote a few lines in the writing pad on his lap while nodding attentively to himself.

Later in the evening he clattered on the Facit at the desk in his room. I knew it was the sound of that book being born. The one about life. The real deal.

And I could tell that this was how it was going to be.

Ulla-Bella's meatballs with potatoes and lingonberries.

Henry and the existential novel.

Edmund and I doing the dishes.

"This is the life," said Edmund when we were almost finished. He sounded moved, and I agreed with him.

"It could have been worse," I said.

But of course Henry had other ideas about how things should be. From the start, it was clear that he'd take the bedroom on the ground floor and that Edmund and I would sleep on the top floor. No discussion needed.

Neither did we need to discuss the fact that the three

of us would have free run of the kitchen and the main room.

"Except," said Henry.

"Except what?" I said.

"Except if I bring a girl back one of these nights. Then the ground floor will be off-limits."

"You bet," I said.

"A gentleman's agreement," said Edmund.

"You cook every other day, and same goes for me. Just dinner, and no baby portions. Same goes for the dishes. Got it?"

"Got it," we said.

"We shop at Laxman's. I'll take Killer, but you can bike or take the boat."

We nodded. No problem.

"The shitter," Henry then said.

"The shitter," we said and sighed.

"The less we shit, the better," said Henry. "And no pissing in it, it's damn bad manners. If we look after it, we can get away with emptying it every other week. You know the deal, Erik … dig a hole, take it out, empty it. I know, there are better jobs. Okay?"

We nodded in earnest.

"That's it," said Henry. "Let's not make life unnecessarily complicated. It should be like a butterfly on a summer's day."

That last bit sounded good. I mulled it over.

Life should be like a butterfly on a summer's day.

There was exactly one month to go before the Incident.

"So, about your toes," I said to Edmund when we went to bed that first night. "What's the deal, anyway?"

Our beds were arranged in the only way possible. Parallel and each along one wall, with the slanted ceiling so close you couldn't sit up. About a meter apart, and a chest of drawers with our clothes inside and tons of comics and books on top. Edmund had sent five shoeboxes full of magazines and one bag of books with Henry.

"My toes?" said Edmund.

"People talk," I said.

"Oh?" said Edmund and giggled. "You can barely see anything anymore." He thrust his left foot out and wiggled his toes. "How many do you see?"

"I count five," I said. "Pretty ugly."

"Correct," said Edmund. "But when I had six, they were even uglier, so they took one away."

"Who?" I said.

"The doctors, of course," said Edmund. "If you look at the index toe or whatever it's called, you can see a small scar at its base. That's where the extra one was."

I got on my knees on the floor and examined Edmund's dirty left foot. What he said was true. Close to the base of the big toe was a small, delicate scratch, thin as a pencil mark and not more than a centimeter long.

I nodded and crawled back into bed.

"Thanks," I said. "I just wanted to see."

"Sure thing," said Edmund and drew his foot back under the blanket. "Do you want to see the other one, too?"

"No need," I said. "Did it hurt?"

"What?"

"When they took them away?"

"Dunno," said Edmund. "I was asleep. I mean, I was under. But it hurt a little after. I was only six."

I nodded. How in the world had anyone found out that he'd had twelve toes, if the eleventh and twelfth had been removed that long ago? He hadn't lived in our town for more than a year.

There was only one explanation. He must have said something.

At first I thought this was strange, but the longer I lay there thinking about it, the more unsure I became.

If I'd had twelve toes would I want to tell people about them? Maybe. Maybe not.

I couldn't decide which and it bothered me. I don't know why.

Like almost every night that followed, we fell asleep to the sound of Henry's typewriter and to the sound of Henry's tape deck.

Elvis. The Shadows.

Buddy Holly, Little Richard, the Drifters.

And to the gentle scratching of tree branches against the window when the wind from the lake blew through the forest.

It felt good.

Almost too good, but then I was being selective about what I was letting in—only what was within reach when we fell asleep at night or when we woke up the next morning.

6

During those first few days at Gennesaret, we surveyed our kingdom.

By sea and by land. Möckeln was about four kilometers across, going by the map. When you were out there rowing the boat, measures of distance felt pointless. Wherever you were going, it would take the time that it took; the important thing was to conserve your energy so you didn't wear out your arms before you got there. In the summertime, there was no need to rush; time was an ocean one thousand times the size of Möckeln, there for you to do with as you pleased.

By the lake, there were really only three destinations. Near its center was Tallön, a barren islet only a couple hundred square meters in size where the seagulls liked to shit. Really there wasn't much there besides bird shit, rocks, and the ten knotted pines growing in a circle in the middle, which had given the place its name. Well, the name it had on the map. Edmund and I called it Shit Island—or Seagull Shit Island: that rolled off the tongue better. With a normal wind it took one rowing session to get there; by "session" we meant that it was too short a trip to bother taking turns at the oars.

It took just about as long to get to Fläskhällen, a small

beach with a café and twenty meters of sandy shore at the north end of the lake. From Gennesaret you could also take the gravel path through the woods, and it was much faster by bike than by boat.

The third destination by boat was Laxman's market in Åsbro. You expected it to take up half of an afternoon if you were doing the shopping—and of course you would be. If you were lucky, Britt would be in the shop. She was also a Laxman, was around our age, and known for being flighty. I wasn't sure what that meant; nor did I know how flightiness found its expression, but she had glittering eyes and plump lips and Edmund said he got a boner just thinking about her.

I didn't like it when Edmund discussed his feelings so plainly. Even if I would freely acknowledge that certain things also gave me an erection, it was a private matter. You didn't just talk about it willy-nilly. Eventually Edmund got the picture. Edmund was good at understanding awkward and sensitive things.

Whatever the case, we agreed that the hours it took to row to Laxman's and retrieve provisions were well spent. We drifted past the area crammed with summer cottages, and the docks, keeping an eye out for suitable girls, even if there rarely were any, and then carried on to Mörk River. It was a lovely river. The reeds were so tall and dense that in some places they were separated by only a meter-wide channel. It was best not to cross paths with a motorboat in this narrow, shimmering green passage—and that our trips down this river bore a striking similarity to what a slow and steady infiltration of the Amazon's swampy jungle would be like, to Edmund and me there was no question.

After a few days, we reached an agreement with Henry that put us in charge of provisions. For the rest of the summer—before what happened happened—Edmund and I journeyed down the Mörk River every second or third day. We took turns rowing, of course. The one who was oarless rested on his belly in the bow of the boat and, with his senses on high alert, he kept an eye out for beaches and watched for the first sign of an approaching crocodile in the quaggy water.

Or a water snake. Or Indians.

Or thought about Britt Laxman.

"*The Log Cabin on the Lingking River,*" said Edmund on one of our first expeditions. "Have you read it?"

"No," I said. "I don't think so."

"Damn good book. It reminds me of this. It's one helluva summer, Erik. Lordy, I hope it never ends."

"Of course it won't," I said. "Toss me a licorice stick."

"Aye aye, Captain," said Edmund. "Do you think Miss Laxman would be interested in a boat trip some time?"

"White man talk crazy," I said. "Laxman is really religious. I'm sure she's chained up behind the counter."

"Hmm," said Edmund. "We'll have to take firearms and a metal saw next time. I can tell by looking at her that she'd be willing to satisfy a young man's every need."

"Only time will tell," I said. This was a sign that I wanted to change the subject, and right on cue Edmund started down another track. Like I said, that Edmund, he was perceptive. Uncommonly perceptive.

Between Gennesaret and the Sjölycke summer resort, there were two so-called real homesteads.

The first, the one nearest to us, was a red shanty down

by the edge of the lake, overgrown with reeds, alders, raspberry thickets, and nettles.

And a lush, untamed forest, as my father would say with a knowing smile that I never fully understood.

When the house was in use, it was inhabited by one or more members of the Lundin family, but it was often empty, because the male Lundins were usually locked up for something or other and the female Lundins were whores or nude dancers or madams and were more at home in an urban environment.

The most famous Lundin was Evert, who had stabbed a cop within an inch of his life when he was only a boy, and later had moved on to bank robberies and arson, as well as racking up numerous assault charges. As far as I could tell, he preferred to assault young women, but if there were none to hand, beating up senior citizens or children would do. It was said that he was illiterate and never learned to tell left from right, no matter how hard he tried, and that said plenty about the Lundin family.

You could say we shared a parking spot with the Lundins, because neither their house nor Gennesaret could be reached by car. Instead, there was a small clearing up the road where cars, bicycles, or mopeds were parked. Then you had to walk down a rugged path for the last hundred meters. One hundred and fifty, if you wanted to get to the Lundins'. But in the other direction, of course. There was a big difference between the Gennesaret path and the Lundin path.

Just as with the narrow and wide ways in the Bible, my mother once explained.

But the Lundin path was both rugged and narrow, so it wasn't really a direct comparison. The other so-called homestead was an old soldier's cottage that lay on a bend off the gravel road that wound through the woods, set a good ways up from the lake. The Levis lived there, an old Jewish couple who had survived Treblinka and who didn't interact with other people. Once a week, they rode down to the village on an old tandem bicycle with a cart that they loaded up at Laxman's with supplies for the next seven days.

At the time I didn't really know what it meant to have survived Treblinka, but I knew that it was so awful you didn't talk about it.

Not my father, not my mother, or anyone else. It seemed as if it might've been better to have died in Treblinka than to have survived it. When I rode past the peaceful cottage in the woods, I wondered if this is what the world was like. Some things were so bad you shouldn't even try to wrap your head around them. You had to just leave them be, allowing them to be unseen and silent, shielded by the words one used to described them nonetheless.

The world, its good and evil, was far bigger than we knew, that I understood, and this fact made me feel oddly calm yet terrified.

I don't know why.

"What's actually the matter with your mom?" Edmund asked one afternoon after we'd biked to Fläskhällen and bought ice cream. We sat by the gray picnic table at the top of the sandy beach, which was empty because it was a cloudy day.

I bit the chocolate coating off my nutty ice-cream bar before I answered.

"Cancer," I said.

"Oh," said Edmund, as if he understood. I don't think he did. Cancer was one of those words. Like Treblinka. Like death. Like fuck.

I didn't want to talk about them. Love? I wondered. Does that belong?

And as we sat there licking our ice cream and looking at the graffiti on the table—all the hearts and the *Cock* and *Cunt* and *Bengt-Göran 22/7/1958*—I repeated the words in my head, the whole chant.

Cancer-Treblinka-Love-Fuck-Death.

All this existed in the world. Existed, existed, existed; and from then on—that whole summer—the chant came to mind occasionally, just those five words, like gibberish. No, not gibberish; more like a kind of incantation against something I understood, but didn't want to understand, I think.

Something shameful, perhaps, that the whole world—not just me—was also ashamed of. A protective language.

Especially when we cycled past the Levis', of course.

Cancer-Treblinka-Love-Fuck-Death.

I needed them, these words. Sometimes I wondered if it was a sign that I was losing my mind.

"Your brother Henry," Edmund said one afternoon. "What's he writing?"

"A book," I said.

"A book?" said Edmund. "Like *Introducing Rex Milligan?*"

That book was part of the library he'd brought with him. We'd both read it a few times already, and agreed that it was a real treat.

Introducing Rex Milligan by Anthony Buckeridge.

"No," I said. "It's something else, I think. Something serious."

Edmund wrinkled his forehead and took off his glasses. They were new for the summer and still in one piece, even though almost a whole week of vacation had already passed.

"There's nothing wrong with being serious," he said. "I'd probably feel more at home in the world if people were a bit more serious."

I'd never heard anyone our age say anything like that, not even the smarty pantses in our class, but when I thought about it, it actually made me happy.

"I guess I would, too," I said.

It was also worrying.

"But seriousness shouldn't be taken too far," Edmund said after a while. "Then you sort of get stuck in it."

"Like in a swamp," I said.

"Exactly like in a swamp," said Edmund.

And that was that.

During the first week out at Gennesaret the weather was varied, but mostly fine. The day we rowed out to Seagull Shit Island and spoke in two-word sentences was scorching, and we dived off the boat and from the island.

"Intolerable heat," said Edmund.

"I agree," I said.

"Fancy rowing?" said Edmund.

"Yes, please," I said.

"Swim now," Edmund said.

"Me, later," I said.

The rules were simple. Every statement had to consist of two words: no more, no less. We alternated each line. If you wanted the other to be quiet, you kept quiet.

"Water cools," I said.

"The feet," said Edmund.

We'd sat down in a crevice where the rocks at our backs were slanted at an accommodating angle. Legs dangling in the water. Picnic basket within reach. Transistor radio on. Dion, if I remember correctly. And Lill-Babs singing "Klas-Göran."

"And legs," I corrected him.

"Cools legs," Edmund agreed.

"Yes, exactly," I said.

"A sandwich?" asked Edmund.

"Not yet."

"Thirsty, then?"

"Yes, please."

"Cheers, brother."

"Cheers, you."

"Good life."

"In deed."

"One word!"

"Two words!"

"In ... deed?"

"Yes, naturally."

"Not indeed?"

It was my turn and to mark that I was tired of splitting hairs, I kept quiet. After a while Edmund started to cough in such an exaggerated way that I was about to say "Shut up!" but I managed to stop myself. Instead I shut my eyes, turned my face to the sun, and controlled the silence between us.

I felt as though I had power over something I couldn't actually have power over. Words. Language.

It felt strange, too. Like when you thought too hard about something.

"Your father?" I asked without opening my eyes.

"My father?" said Edmund.

"Has magazines?" I said.

"You mean?" said Edmund.

"Special magazines," I elaborated.

Edmund sighed wearily.

"Special magazines," he said.

I considered his tone.

"My apologies," I said.

Edmund stretched one foot up to the sky and spread his toes. The delicate scar made a rare appearance.

"No need," he said.

"Rumbling stomach," I said.

"Mine, too," said Edmund.

Henry came up and woke us on Saturday morning.

"I'm going into town," he said. "You'll be fine here; there's hot dogs and mashed potatoes for dinner. I'll be late, so you'll have to fix it yourselves."

"What are you up to?" I asked.

Henry shrugged and lit a Lucky.

"Gotta take care of a few things. By the way ..."

"Yes?"

"Are you going to Lacka Park tonight?"

"Maybe," I said. "Why?"

Henry took a few drags and seemed to be thinking.

"We need a signal," he said.

"A signal?" said Edmund.

Edmund didn't usually get involved when Henry and I were talking, and Henry looked at him with mock surprise.

"If I get lucky," he said.

"Aha," I said.

"I get you," said Edmund.

"Listen," Henry said after taking a couple more drags on the fag. "If there's a tie around the flagpole, that means you go right up to bed if you come home later than I do. Okay?"

Edmund and I looked at each other.

"No objection," said Edmund. "A tie on the flagpole."

"All right," said Henry, and disappeared.

A swath of smoke and irritation lingered in the room. We lay there, waiting for it to disperse. We heard Henry slam the door downstairs and walk up the path.

"Your brother doesn't like me," said Edmund after a few minutes.

I didn't know how to respond to that.

"Of course he does," I said. "Why wouldn't he?"

"It's fine," said Edmund. "You don't have to pretend."

Cancer-Treblinka-Love-Fuck-Death, I thought. Why would I pretend?

"I don't know what you're talking about," I said and went out and sat on the toilet.

7

We hung around the Sjölycke jetties for an hour on our first Saturday morning, but it was mostly grown-ups and kids splashing around and pissing in the water, so at noon we decided to row out to Shit Island.

I'd pinched six Lucky Strikes from a couple of Henry's many open packets, and we lay there surrounded by bird poop, drinking apple juice and smoking while we listened to *Sveriges bilradio*, a radio show for drivers, and the summer hit parade. It was as hot as it had been in the previous days and Edmund's back was already starting to peel. We played the two-word-sentence game, but got bored, and we didn't really talk about anything.

As I said, silence wasn't a problem with Edmund. We lay there smoking, sharing cigarette after cigarette, and passing bottles of juice between us. We were almost like an old married couple who'd spent their whole lives together and had no need for words anymore.

No pressing need, anyway.

On the whole, it felt pretty good.

"Do you think about your life?" Edmund asked after we'd lain around for a few minutes listening to "Young World" with our eyes closed in the sun, digging it, as the waves lapped at our calves. Edmund and I both thought that "Young World" was a bonafide hit, no doubt, almost on par with "Cotton Fields."

"My life?" I said. "How do you mean?"

"You know, what it's like," Edmund said. "Compared to other lives."

"No," I said. "I guess I don't really think about that."

"If it could've been different somehow," Edmund went on.

I paused before I said:

"You only have one life. The one you have. I don't see what good it would do to dream about anything else."

Edmund drank some juice and scratched the bridge of his nose, as he did when he wasn't wearing his glasses.

"I mean, what if you had different parents?"

I didn't answer.

"How's it really going with your mom?"

"The cancer," I said after a while. "It is what it is."

"Is she going to die?" Edmund said.

"No one knows," I said.

"Us and our moms," Edmund said, laughing.

"What do you mean by that?" I said.

"They're similar," said Edmund. "Yours has the cancer and mine has the bottle."

"They're not alike at all," I said. "They are actually really different."

My irritation didn't pass Edmund by. When he started talking again, he'd changed his tone.

"She's drying out this summer, my mom is."

I only vaguely knew what he meant.

"Drying out?"

"Vissingsberg," said Edmund. "The whole summer. She's going to learn to live without alcohol; she's done it a few times already. That's why it was such a good thing for me to be able to come out here with you. Didn't you know?"

"No," I said. "But I don't see why it matters. If we're going to talk, let's talk about something else."

"Okay," said Edmund.

I knew he would have wanted to keep talking about his alcoholic mom, but I didn't. Instead we lay there and listened to the rest of the summer hit parade, smoked the last Lucky, and rowed back to Gennesaret to eat hot dogs and mashed potatoes and to fix ourselves up for the night ahead.

We'd figured out that if we ate enough at home we wouldn't have to spend our cash on hot dogs in Lacka Park. So we ate the whole fifteen-pack of Sibylla; Edmund eight, me seven. And six portions of instant mashed potatoes. I felt queasy afterward, but Edmund said he was on top form. We took a quick dip off the side of the boat—the pontoon dock wasn't finished yet and it was tricky getting in from the shore—whacked a little Brylcreem in our hair, pulled on clean nylon shirts, and rode off on our bikes through the woods.

It wasn't more than five kilometers from Gennesaret to Lacka Park, but we took a few wrong turns and it was an hour before we arrived.

This early summer evening was like early summer evenings were at that time. Rich with perfume and promise. Equal parts lilac, jasmine, and moonshine. At least around Lacka Park. We agreed that it was dumb to spend three kronor on admission and parked our bikes a ways into the woods. We chained them together too; we couldn't have some drunk steeling our bikes, leaving us to walk home in the middle of the night. You never knew.

Outside the entrance we bumped into Lasse Side-Smile, whose parents had a cottage in Sjölycke. Side-Smile was a little older than us, had left Stava School a few years back, and his nickname came from his deformed head. Part of the lower half of his face was just sort of missing and when he spoke it looked like he was trying to whisper in his own ear. I didn't know him particularly well. No one did; he usually kept to himself, whether on account of his looks or something else, I don't know.

"Mad Dog Raffe is on duty," he said, looking worried and even more deformed.

"Oh crap," I said.

When Mad Dog Raffe was working it was hard to get in without paying. There were spots where you could slip through the decaying wooden plank fence that surrounded the fairground—especially behind the stinking "conveniences" in the most densely wooded corner—but Mad Dog Raffe was known for his ability to tell at a glance which visitors hadn't paid for admission. And because this was probably his only talent, he liked making the most of it. When he found some underage kid who couldn't show him a valid ticket, he was especially intimidating and stubborn. Not to mention heavy-handed. That's why he was in demand as a security guard; I could hardly imagine him taking payment for it, either. The uniform seemed to be payment enough. Whatever the case, there was no point in arguing with Mad Dog Raffe; saying you'd paid but lost the ticket was about as futile as talking back to the police when they caught you riding your bike without lights.

"You gonna pay?" Lasse Side-Smile wondered.

Edmund and I dug into our pockets and counted our cash.

"I don't know," I said. "Are there any people in there?"

"Tons," said Lasse Side-Smile. "The hell with it. I'll take my chances. I'm out of money anyway."

Edmund and I decided to compromise. I would pay, and Edmund would hang back with Side-Smile behind the urinals. Mad Dog Raffe didn't really know who Edmund was because he was new in town, but he knew me more than well. He'd kicked both Benny and me out of Tajkon Filipson's World Famous Fun Fair at Hammarberg's field just under a month ago.

This logic proved to be sound. Half an hour later, Mad Dog Raffe came over as the three of us were hanging around the shooting gallery. Edmund slipped away and I showed him my yellow ticket with restrained triumph and Lasse Side-Smile was kicked out with a ruckus.

"You shithead, you belong in the loony bin!" he shouted when he was a safe distance down the road.

Mad Dog Raffe just grinned and packed in more snus under his lip. He rolled his yellow eyes, straightened his uniform and slid into the crowd, on the hunt for new victims.

Duty above all.

I'd only visited Lacka Park twice before, both times were during last summer. There wasn't actually much for Edmund and me to do there. The dancing, necking, and drinking were more for an older crowd.

But there was enough to interest us flashes of what life had in store in a few years' time. In addition to dancing and necking, that is.

Take the poker tent, for instance. We made a beeline for it as soon as Lasse Side-Smile was out of the picture. The smoky den was crowded with dozens of local talents trying to beat poker pro Harry Diamond and his wife, Vicky Diamond. They were quite the attraction. You could feel the heat of their sins burning in your trousers as you neared the tent.

The game was a variation of stud poker; Harry played against three or four others at a time and Vicky dealt. She handled those cards like she was born with a deck in her hands, and it was impossible to tell if she was dealing from the top or the bottom. When the game was at a critical junction, she'd lean so far forward that her burnished breasts threatened to spill from her dress, and when that happened, no one could keep their eyes on the cards. Everyone playing the game knew this trick, but it made no difference. Your eyes glued themselves to her cans and you got taken for a ride, and that was that.

On this particular evening we watched Big Anton, Balthazar Lindblom's older brother, lose fifty kronor in under fifteen minutes, and later a fat egg-seller from Hjortkvarn stormed out of the tent, promising to return to cut the balls off Harry and the boobs off Vicky.

After the poker tent, we went to the arcade. Even with a mere eight one-armed bandits under the sagging tarp, we still managed to lose our two kronor in the bat of an eye, and it was then—as we slunk out of the tent feeling low—that we saw Ewa Kaludis.

She was standing all alone between the arcade tent and the dance floor, smoking a cigarette. Her dress was white, the bag hanging nonchalantly on her shoulder was also white, and I understood in an instant why she was on her own in this sea of people.

She was just too beautiful. Like a goddess or a Kim Novak. You can't fly too close to the sun, and everyone who saw her on that summer's eve knew it. The park had started to fall into shadow, particularly where the glow of the lanterns could not reach, and Ewa Kaludis was standing in one of these darker spots. Even so, she seemed to have a shimmer about her—like an angel—or to be painted with one of those luminescent colors that Mr. Jonsson used for the snowmen on the window of his toy store for the Christmas display in December.

We stopped dead in our tracks.

"Huh," said Edmund.

I said nothing. I shut my eyes tightly and mustered the courage to walk up to her. The seconds felt like an eternity, and when I reached her, it felt like I had aged.

"Hi, Ewa," I said with more nerve than Colonel Darkin and Yuri Gagarin had put together.

She lit up.

"Well, hello," she murmured. "Fancy seeing you here."

Her warmth left me speechless, but Edmund, only two steps behind, came to my rescue.

"Of course we are," he answered. "Has Madam been left all on her lonesome?"

I felt a pang of envy for not having come up with a line like that myself. Masculine and protective yet cheeky.

She laughed and took a drag of her cigarette.

"I'm waiting for my fiancé," she said.

"And where is he?" Edmund asked.

She shrugged, and right then Berra Albertsson stepped out of the dark together with Atle Eriksson, another handball player. They had their arms around each other's shoulders and were making a show of laughing at something. They'd obviously gone behind the tent for a pee and a tipple. Berra let go of Atle and put his arm around Ewa Kaludis. Then he fixed his eyes on us.

"So who are these ankle-biters?" he asked.

Atle Eriksson guffawed and a mist of schnapps blasted from his mouth.

"Erik and Edmund," said Ewa Kaludis. "I got to know

them at Stava. They're lovely boys."

"I'm sure they are," Super-Berra replied, pulling her closer to him. "But it's high time we dance. Later, you little shits!"

"Goodbye," Edmund and I said in unison. And then they disappeared. We stood there, watching them go.

"What a prick," said Edmund. "I don't know what she sees in him."

"Me neither," I said. "Who knows what goes on in women's heads?"

"It's like he's asking for punch in the face," Edmund added.

"Exactly," I said.

We wandered around Lacka Park for another few hours, clearly Britt Laxman had other plans that night, and we got rid of what little money we had as slowly as we could. Cotton candy. The Chocolate Spin 'n' Win. A Loranga soda and a pricey waffle with whipped cream and raspberry jam.

Just as we were about to make our way back to Gennesaret, we realized we weren't the only ones that night who wanted to sock Super-Berra one.

There hadn't been a lot of fighting going on, but the time had come. It was in the air. Edmund and I had just been behind the dance floor smoking the last of the three Lucky Strikes I'd nabbed from Henry, when we ran into the whole gang.

Or rather, the gangs. The fighters and their back-up. On one side, Super-Berra, Atle Eriksson, and a few reeling handball players. On the other, a cocky, red-faced man whom I'd never seen before. He was tattooed from head to toe and looked dangerous. And his entourage: half a dozen men just like him.

"You're gonna get what's coming to you, you no-good handball-playing ape!" slurred the red-faced one and tried to pull himself free from his back-up.

"Calm down, Mulle," one of them insisted. "You'll get your shot at that darkie, but we have to lay low ... the cops, and all."

Mulle gave an assured nod. I didn't get what he meant by "darkie"; Super-Berra did have dark hair and a buzz cut, but he wasn't black.

He was silent. Seemed calm and collected, and when everyone was shielded from view by the tent, he handed his striped blazer to one of the handball players, ceremoniously rolled up his sleeves, got into position, and waited. Legs planted far apart, his guard up, and a smirk on his face. His knees were slightly bent and he was swaying, gently rocking from side to side, fists loose. I noticed I was holding my breath and Edmund was pressed up against me, grinding his teeth from all the anticipation. Other than the two gangs, Edmund and I were the only onlookers; the arena for the fight had been carefully chosen, no doubt about it. I shut my eyes and took a deep breath. The night air was full of summer and schnapps. I wondered where Ewa Kaludis was right then. "Twilight Time" spilled from the dance floor, it was getting late.

And then Mulle's buddies sent him on his way. He let out an impressive roar—"Aaarrgh!"—tucked his head, and charged at Super-Berra. Even in the heat of the moment, I knew this was a terrible tactic. All Berra needed to do was move aside—a "sidestep" as it's called in boxing—use Mulle's own momentum against him, and strike.

And that's exactly what he did, but he didn't stop there. The red-faced Mulle doubled over like a clubbed ox after that first punch, then Berra lifted him up by the collar and walloped him three or four more times before turning him around and bashing his head into the ground, twice, with all his might.

My stomach lurched each time Mulle's head made impact, and when it was done, a hush had fallen over the fighters. Mulle's buddies and the handball players were dumbstruck, and when Super-Berra straightened up and gestured for his blazer, Atle Eriksson handed it over without a word. Then they turned their backs on Mulle and walked off.

Solemnly. Like after a funeral or something. Edmund and I slunk away. I felt ashamed for some reason and Edmund did too, I guess, because neither of us said a word until we were out of the park and unlocking our bikes.

"That was grim," Edmund said, and I thought I heard his voice tremble.

"And unfair," I said. "Damned unfair. You don't hit a man when he's down."

As we biked home through the woods, I wondered where Ewa Kaludis had been during the fight and if being like Berra Albertsson was how you won over a woman like her.

I remember crying quietly as we trundled through the mild June night.

Yes, it was the middle of the night, the rear wheel of Edmund's bike chirring and me crying quietly without knowing why.

8

On Sunday, my dad came to visit. He didn't stay long because he'd got a lift from Ivar Bäck, who was helping someone in Sjölycke with their TV antenna.

We sat outside on the lawn for an hour, ate the watery strawberries he'd brought with him, and talked, but not much. Things with my mother could have been worse, my father said. She was going in for another series of tests. It would take a few weeks. A month, maybe.

And then we'd see.

Only time would tell.

Henry offered to drive our father home in Killer on his way into town later that evening, but our dad just shook his head.

"I'll go with Bäck," he said. "No fuss that way."

Afterward, Edmund asked what he meant by that. Why it would be less fuss going with Bäck.

I shrugged.

"He thinks Henry drives like a madman," I said. "He can barely stand being in a car with him."

When my father was on his way, I noticed he hadn't asked about Emmy Kaskel. Maybe Henry had told him after all.

"Buddy," said Edmund when he'd finished reading *Colonel Darkin and the Golden Ewes*. "This is really something. You're going to be a millionaire."

I'd finished *Colonel Darkin and the Golden Ewes* before we went out to Gennesaret, and I'd brought it with me, along with a new notebook. For a rainy day, or if the spirit moved me.

The spirit moved me, but it was impossible to keep the comic-drawing a secret from Edmund. After some deliberation, I'd left the notebook out with the other books half by chance, and it wasn't long before Edmund spotted it. And it wasn't much longer before he read it.

"It's not really any good," I said. "No need to pretend."

"Not any good!" Edmund said. "It's the best damn thing I've seen since Grandma got her tits caught in the mangler!"

This was a saying from Norrland, and was meant to convey the highest praise and appreciation. I couldn't contain my joy.

"Oh," I said. "Shit on you, you squirt."

This was another saying from Norrland.

The spirit that moved me to draw definitely had something to do with what happened on Saturday night in Lacka Park. I needed to draw and tell a story about a woman like Ewa Kaludis; it was like an ache in me. Maybe I wanted to get a few of my own punches in—but in a cleaner way than in the fight I'd witnessed between Super-Berra and red-faced Mulle. The day after, we'd started to discuss how Mulle might be doing, but both Edmund and I got the chills when we thought about what his face must look like now. Not to mention how his head must be feeling.

In any case, there were a few rain showers on Sunday evening, and while Edmund was on his bed trying to write a letter to his mother in Vissingsberg, I was on mine, drawing the first panels of Colonel Darkin and the Mysterious Heiress.

I remember thinking what a pleasant evening it was.

The deeper into summer we got, the more my brother Henry was consumed with his existential novel. He was nigh on secretive about it. He often slept long into the day, got up and took a dip in the lake, and sat down by the typewriter with coffee and a cigarette. Preferably out on the lawn by the wobbly table, weather permitting. Which it did, for the most part. When the question of supper arose, he almost always talked his way out of kitchen duty and tossed Edmund and me five or ten kronor to take care of it: secure provisions, cook, and do the dishes.

It was no skin off our backs. Though money was tight, our basic needs were met, and it was nice to be able to buy an ice cream now and again. At Laxman's or by Fläskhällen. Or a few loose cigarettes; we couldn't always be pilfering them from Henry, even if he probably never would have noticed.

After dinner Henry would disappear in Killer, and at least two out of three evenings Edmund and I would be in bed before he returned. Sometimes I woke up in the middle of the night to the sound of the Facit's clatter and the tape deck playing Eddie Cochran. The Drifters. Elvis Presley. He'd recorded "Wooden Heart" on several places on the tape. When the music ended, the birds singing in the bushes under the window took over. Sometimes I asked Henry how it was going with his book, but he never felt like talking about it. "It's going," he'd say and take a drag from one of his eternal Luckys.

It's going.

In a low-key sort of way, I was curious about what he was writing, but he never left any papers out and I didn't want to ask him more than once. One night, just after he'd driven away in Killer, I happened to catch sight of a sheet still in the machine on the desk. There were just a few lines on it; gingerly, I sat down on the chair and turned the roller up a few notches so it would be easier to read.

I must have read the text five or six times. Maybe because I thought it was good, but also because it was so unexpected. Unexpected and eerie:

rushes him from behind, stopping at just the right distance. A step forward across the gravel, no more than one, hand tightly gripping the shaft, and then the brief fatal blow. When steel meets skull the sound that is born is mute. The inverse of a sound, audible because it is more silent than silence, and when the heavy body meets the earth the thick summer night smiles wryly; everything slips into everything else and

He'd stopped there. I twisted the roller back, feeling like a thief in the night. As Benny's mother would say.

Cancer-Treblinka-Love-Fuck-Death, I thought. What sort of book are you writing, brother?

It took a few days to plan our night raid on Karlesson's shop, and on Thursday, the day before Midsummer's Eve, we did the deed. Henry had apparently decided to stay home that night, but we said we had business to attend to in the evening and shortly after nine we were on our way. Henry didn't seem to care.

"If you get up to no good, make sure you don't get caught," he said without looking up from his typewriter.

We took four apple juices and a baguette as provisions, and just over ten kronor, so we could each buy a hot-dog special at Törner's on the square before he closed at eleven.

At first all went as planned. It was a blustery night; a headwind was charging over the plain, but we pulled into the square in Kumla around quarter to eleven. Rain was in the air and there was barely a soul on the street. After we'd eaten our sausages and drained our apple juices, Törner sputtered home in his food truck and we searched for spoons. After we'd combed the square we carried on to the trash cans outside Pressbyrån by the station and around the other hot-dog stand in town: Herman's by the apartment buildings. By midnight we thought we had enough: fifty-three pieces. If you could expect about three gumballs and one plastic deal per twist, it would all add up to one hundred and fifty balls and fifty-three plastic deals.

But we couldn't possibly manage to chew all that gum and there probably wasn't more than that in Karlesson's dispenser anyway. Cautiously, we pedaled the last two hundred meters south along Mossbanegatan. Nothing crossed out path. Not even a cat. It started drizzling. We were looking forward to working undisturbed during the small hours, no question. I was buzzing with anticipation, and the excitement made Edmund giddy. We braked in front of the slumbering kiosk.

There were two handwritten notes on the empty glass container. On one it said "Broken," on the other "Not in servis." Karlesson wasn't known for his spelling.

I stared at the dispenser for a few seconds. Then I saw red. I wasn't normally one to lose my cool, but I couldn't get a handle on my rage.

"Damn fucking Cunt-Karlesson!" I screamed, and then

I kicked the iron pole that the glass jar was mounted on as hard as I could.

I was only wearing flimsy blue sneakers and the pain shooting from the now broken toe was so intense I thought I was going to faint.

"Calm down," Edmund said. "You'll wake the whole town, you ape."

I moaned and slid down the wall of the kiosk.

"Aw, hell, I think I broke a toe," I whined. "How the hell could the damned dispenser be broken tonight of all nights? It hasn't been broken in three years."

"Does it hurt?" Edmund wondered.

"Like all hell," I said through clenched teeth.

But the first wave of bright white pain was already receding. I pulled off my shoe and tried to wiggle my toes. It didn't go well.

"God's finger," said Edmund after watching my wiggling for a moment.

"What?" I said.

"The fact that the dispenser is kaput," said Edmund. "It must mean that we weren't supposed to raid it tonight. It wasn't meant to be, you know. God's finger. That's what it's called."

I had a hard time being interested in anyone's finger with my toe hurting so much, but I suspected Edmund had a point.

"Is there another dispenser in town?" he asked.

I thought about it.

"Not outside. They have one inside Svea's, I think."

"Hmm," said Edmund. "What should we do?"

I tried to put my shoe back on. I couldn't, so I shoved it in my backpack and opened an apple juice instead. Edmund sank down next to me and we each took a sip.

That's when the police car showed up.

The black-and-white Amazon came to a stop right in front of us and the driver rolled down the window.

"What are you two up to?"

I was speechless, even more speechless than when I'd been face-to-face with Ewa Kaludis in Lacka Park. More speechless than a dead herring. Edmund got up.

"My friend hurt his foot," he said. "We're on our way home."

"Is it serious?" asked the policeman.

"No, we can manage," Edmund said.

"We'll give you a ride if you need one."

"Thank you so much," Edmund said. "Maybe another time."

I stood up to show that everything was indeed fine.

"All right," said the policeman. "Hurry on home now, it's late."

And then they drove away. We hung back until their red taillights were out of sight. Then, Edmund said:

"See? God works in mysterious ways. Now tell me, is there another dispenser in Hallsberg?"

We made off with 166 balls, 45 rings, and 20-something invaluable plastic thingies from the chewing-gum dispenser by the train station kiosk at Hallsberg. It went smoothly; it was five past two according to the station clock by the time we were done and my toe didn't hurt at all anymore. It was stiff and swollen and numb, but what the hell did that matter when you had a week's worth of gum?

Edmund didn't try to conquer Kleva that night. Instead, we walked all the way up the hill, which took a while on account of my broken toe. Over the next few days, I'd learn that it was much easier to ride a bike than it was to walk.

On the home stretch, from Åsbro and through the forest, it began to pour, and by the time we tossed our bikes aside in the parking area, we were beat. In addition to Killer and a few of the Lundins' old motorbikes, a moped was parked up there. A red Puch. If I hadn't been soaked-through and so tired, I might've recognized it.

When we reached the house, the rain stopped. The sun was on its way up and one of Henry's ties was knotted around the flagpole.

9

On the afternoon of Midsummer's Eve, both of our dads came out to visit for a few hours. Mr. Wester was full of summer cheer; in addition to herring and new potatoes he brought a bundle of blue and yellow paper flags and an accordion. The weather wasn't bad; we ate at the table out on the lawn while he played us a few tunes. "The Rush of the Avesta Rapids," "Afternoon at Möljaren," and a couple more I didn't recognize. As well as one of his own compositions called "For Signe."

As he played it, tears welled in his eyes, and I was struck by the absence of women in our lives. "Eight-sixed," as Karlesson would say when you wanted something he didn't have in stock.

Five men sitting around celebrating Midsummer as best they could, and I tried to project myself into the future. What would it be like in ten years? Would my father and Edmund's father be all alone then? Would Henry have settled down and had a family? And Edmund? That was hard to picture. Edmund with a wife and children! Four six-toed tiny Edmunds with broken glasses.

And me?

"What sadness," Edmund's dad said and put the accordion aside. "As with life, so with summer. It's only just begun and suddenly it's autumn. So sad."

But then he laughed out loud and helped himself to more herring and potatoes.

"Truer words were never spoken," said my father.

Henry sighed and lit a Lucky Strike.

They left us around five, our fathers; they'd only borrowed their colleague's car for the afternoon and were both working the evening shift at the prison. Edmund's dad suggested they pick nine kinds of flowers to put under their pillows, but my father was none too amused by the idea.

"We already know which women we'll be dreaming of," he said with a half-hearted smile. Then they waved goodbye and walked up to the parking spot.

Edmund and I had decided to check out Fläskhällen, where they usually celebrated Midsummer by raising a maypole, dancing, the whole kit and caboodle. He'd be damned, Edmund said, if Britt Laxman didn't turn up at a place like that, and as soon as we were done with the dishes we climbed in the boat and rowed away. When we were out on the lake, Edmund said:

"Were you awake at all last night?"

"Awake?" I said. "What do you mean?"

"Well, maybe you heard something."

"Heard what?"

Edmund stopped rowing.

"Your brother, of course. And that chick, whoever she is. They were going at it."

"I see," I said and tried to sound uninterested. "No, I was sleeping like a log."

Edmund looked at me hesitantly and we didn't speak for a while.

"Should we switch places?" I asked when we'd gone about halfway.

"No, no," said Edmund. "You need to rest your toe."

"My toe won't be doing the rowing," I said.

But Edmund didn't let go of the oars. The music from Fläskhällen grew louder. I was resting on the stern thwart, running my hand through the water, trying to not think about what'd I'd missed out on in the night.

Or in the morning, which it must have been. We hadn't gone to bed until after three and not a sound was coming from Henry's room then.

I couldn't really get my thoughts in order; while it was quite arousing to know that my brother might've been having sex with a girl right under our floorboards, it was disgraceful somehow, too. As if Edmund had unearthed an indecent family secret. As if I should feel ashamed of what Henry was up to. Of course thinking along these lines stunk, I'd be the first to admit that. If there was one thing in this world I envied it was the ability to find yourself a girl and get what you wanted from her. That was what life was all about, wasn't it? Life and everything.

I slipped my whole arm into the water, trying as hard as I could to think about something else, but it was tough going, like I said. Edmund rowed along, carefree, and didn't seem to be trying to think of anything else. To the contrary.

"This is a brilliant summer, Erik," he said as we approached the channel of reeds. "In every way. It's probably the best I've had."

I was struck by how much I liked Edmund. There were only two weeks to go until the Incident, my mother was dying of cancer, my toe was busted, but yes, it really was a brilliant summer.

In every way. So far.

Neither Edmund nor I thought that Midsummer at Fläskhällen was a winner. Sure, Britt Laxman was one of the first people we saw as we pulled up in the boat, but she was being escorted by some redhead wearing sunglasses and winklepickers, otherwise there wasn't much there. A few drunks in sports clothes were sitting around drinking coffee spiked with moonshine. The three-man band was on a break when we arrived. They really should have kept taking it easy all night. They played the accordion, guitar, and a double bass that seemed to be strung with old rubber bands. Four couples pretended to dance along, some wearing clogs, some not, some to the music, some not, and a few scattered groups of people around our age were hanging around trying to look like President Kennedy or his First Lady. We played a round of golf and tried to get in with two giggling Jackie-alikes from Skåne, but they soon retreated to their families' trailers, which were set up over by the camping tents.

The campsite wasn't exactly big, but it was by no means full: four trailers, as many sagging tents, and a half-dozen cows who either had taken the wrong route or had been brought there as lawnmowers by the farmer, Grundberg, who also took care of the rigamarole at Fläskhällen beach.

Inside the café was a new pinball machine. It was called a Rocket 2000; we tried our best to have a turn, but a group of kids from Askersund who had arrived on mopeds seemed to have a flood of one-krona coins to pour into the machine. In the end we decided to postpone the game. Shortly thereafter we saw Britt Laxman and the red-haired boy sitting down by the fire on the beach grilling sausages on the same stick, so we gave up and rowed back to Gennesaret.

My father had taught me that there's no point plowing

on when the odds are against you, and Edmund agreed wholeheartedly.

"When the going gets tough, the tough get going, you bastard son of a loose mosquito," he'd said. He'd insisted that was the kind of thing you said man-to-man deep in the forests of Hälsingland, and I had no reason not to believe him.

When we were out on the water, Edmund told me a secret. He started by asking a question.

"Have you ever been beaten up? I mean taken a real pounding."

I don't think so, I said. I'd never been given more than a slap or an Indian burn or an accidental blow to the solar plexus. Or a few whacks with Benny's hockey stick after I broke it by accident because I didn't look where I was sitting.

"I have," Edmund said gravely. "When I was little. By my dad. A helluva lot."

"Your dad? What are you talking about? Why would your dad—?"

"Not him," Edmund interrupted. "The other one, my real dad. Albin is just my stepdad; he married Mum after my real dad disappeared. Boy, he let rip ... on Mom and me. Once he hit Mom so hard she lost her hearing."

"Why?" I asked. I didn't know what else to say.

Edmund shrugged.

"He was like that." He thought for a moment. "You never forget. How it feels. How ... how scared you get, lying there, waiting. Waiting is almost worse than the beating itself."

"I understand," I said. "Is that why your mom is an alcoholic?"

"I think so," said Edmund and dipped his glasses in

the water to rinse them clean. "He drank like there was no tomorrow, and taught her how ... but she was born with a pedigree. Grandpa drank enough for an entire platoon."

"Where's he now, your real dad?"

"No idea," said Edmund. "He disappeared when I was five and a half; Mom refuses to talk about him. Albin came into the picture pretty quick after that."

I nodded.

"To hell with people who fight," Edmund said as he put his dripping glasses back on. "Who prey on the weak. I can't stand it."

"It sucks," I agreed. "You shouldn't have to stand for it."

Henry was gone by the time we got back and we spent the rest of the night playing Chinese chequers and chewing gum. We came up with our own variation where we played using gumballs. There was something about having to chew your opponent's gum if you jumped over it, but we never quite settled on the rules. We went to bed early; we hadn't slept much the night before, especially Edmund, and we couldn't care less about putting flowers under our pillows and all that romantic nonsense.

I drew a few panels of my comic before I fell asleep, and Edmund wrote a letter to his mother at Vissingsberg. He hadn't been happy with his previous drafts, and now he was trying a lighter, more masculine approach. When he was finished, he tore the page right out of his notebook and handed it to me.

"What do you think?" he said chewing his pen.

It read:

Mornin', Mom!
I'm having a gay old time out here. I hope you're sober
and are as happy as a clam. See you in the fall.
Your one and only Edmund

"It's great," I said. "She's going to frame it and hang it over her bed."

"I think so too," said Edmund.

Not a single sound came from downstairs that night, not even from the tape deck or the typewriter, but at some point towards morning I woke to the sound of firecrackers being shot off and rockets being launched over at the Lundins'. Apparently, they were having some sort of family gathering; we hadn't heard a peep from them for two weeks, but it was just like them to announce themselves in this way. And on Midsummer's Eve, too.

Anyway, I fell back asleep, and had a strange dream about Henry getting his tie caught in the typewriter. He was frantically pounding on the keys trying to get free, but with each line the tie was pulled tighter. In the end—when his nose was practically on the roller—he called for help. Well, it was more of a hiss because he could barely breathe. I cut off the tie, and as thanks he slapped me and explained it was a damn expensive tie and I'd ruined an entire chapter for him.

Even as I was dreaming, I thought it was strange, and when I woke up I was still mad at Henry. It was rotten of him to slap me after I'd saved his life. It didn't matter if it was a dream or reality: it was unfair.

But when I got up, he was already sitting on the lawn, writing and smoking. In just his underwear and without any sign of a tie; it must have just been one of those dreams that had gotten out of hand. Meaningless, no matter how you turned it around. I went out to him.

"How's it going?" I asked. "With the book."

He leaned back and squinted at the sun, which had just broken through the clouds.

"Rolling along," he said. "It's rolling along, little brother."

And then he laughed that short, sharp laugh of his and went on clattering.

I hesitated before asking, "Did you find yourself a new girl?"

He typed until it pinged at the end of the line.

"I'm working on it," he said and looked pensive. "Yes indeed. There's a lot I'm working on."

I couldn't figure out what he meant, so I asked.

"It means everything," my brother said, then laughed again. "Everything."

10

During the last week of June it was so hot the outhouse barrel was boiling.

At least it felt that way if you forgot to cover it properly with peat moss litter; there was a distinct advantage in waiting to go until the evening.

The need to cool off by taking dips in the lake became much more pressing—as well as the need to finish the pontoon dock. Pushing the boat out every time you wanted to take a dip was too involved, and none of us— neither I nor Edmund nor Henry—was especially fond of teetering around on the sticky bottom where you might find yourself sinking down knee-deep in a mud hole or tripping on a root and landing on your face.

So, the dock. It was about time. We'd already transported six empty barrels from Laxman's and Henry had sketched it out. Hammers, ropes, nails, and saws were stored in the shed by the outhouse. All we needed was wood.

Planks.

"The Lundins," said Henry when the sun was high in the sky of a new day, hotter than Marilyn Monroe's kisses. "You're going to have to nab a few planks from the Lundins' pile."

"Us?" I said.

"You," said Henry. "I'm up to my ears. You want a dock, don't you?"

"Of course," I said.

"All right, then," said Henry. He put on the old straw hat he'd bought at a flea market in Beirut and rejoined his typewriter in the shade. "Twenty kronor if you're done before nightfall!" he called out from his chair. "Shouldn't be a problem for two sharpshooters."

"Who says it's a problem?" said Edmund. "What a load of crap."

But he said it quietly, certain Henry couldn't hear.

The Lundins' timber stockpile lay next to the path down to their house, not more than ten meters from the parking spot up by the road. It was a considerable pile, hidden by an old, moldy tarp, and it had lain there as long as I could remember. Most likely it had been lifted from a building site a long time ago and they couldn't be bothered to carry it any further than just out of sight from the road—and most likely none of them would care in the slightest if a few planks went missing from the pile.

Especially if they didn't notice.

The safest thing would have been to launch our mission in the small hours. But you never really knew with the Lundins. They had their own circadian rhythm. It was also clear that they'd arrived for the summer now. At least a few of them had; we'd heard a bit of a ruckus over the past days: cursing, glass breaking, and all that.

Another reason not to go at night was of course those twenty kronor on the line, so we really just had to pull ourselves up by the bootstraps and get on with it. No hesitation, no objections: Edmund and I agreed on that point.

You could say our mission was a success. For a few hours, we dragged planks through the marshy, inhospitable mosquito and gadfly hell that lay between the Lundins and Gennesaret. We swore and were pricked by thorns, swore and were bitten, swore and made our way down. Got scratched up and bruised all over. The heat drove us mad, but we did it. We made it.

By twelve thirty we'd amassed a respectable pile of planks, which Henry—leaning back, lifting his hat, squinting, and lighting a Lucky Strike—deemed sufficient.

"That'll do," he said. "Need a hand building it? It'll cut into your fee, obviously."

"Like hell we do," we said.

We sawed and hammered and fastened, and talked about Edmund's real dad. And about why he was so violent. Because it seemed strange—at least to me.

"He was sick," said Edmund. "He had a unusual brain disorder. When he drank, he had to fight."

"Sustained," I said. "Why did he drink?"

"That was another part of the illness," Edmund suggested. "He simply had to have alcohol. Or else he'd go nuts. Yup, that's how it was ..."

I considered what he said.

"So, either he went nuts or he went nuts?"

"Exactly," said Edmund. "That's how it is for some people. It's a shame it had to be my dad."

"A crying shame," I said. "He shouldn't have been a dad at all."

Edmund nodded.

"But it wasn't like that in the beginning. Before I was born. The illness came creeping ... then it was what it was."

"Hmm," I said. "Is it hereditary?"

"Don't know."

A few seconds passed.

"But I hate him anyway," Edmund said with rising anger. "It's damn cowardly to attack people who can't defend themselves. And with a belt … Why did he have to use the belt, can you tell me that?"

I couldn't.

"Hitting a person when they're down—"

He stopped there. I pictured Mulle unconscious, his ruddy face, and recalled how Super-Berra had lifted it up and bashed it into the ground. "Mm," I said. "There's nothing worse. Do you think you'll look him up when you get older? Your real dad. Track him down and corner him?"

"Yessir," said Edmund. "You can count on it. For that reason alone I hope he's still alive. I have it all worked out. First I'm going to find him and not tell him who I am, then I'm going to be nice to him, sweeter than honey, buy him a coffee and some cake … and a drink … and when he least expects it I'll tell him who I am and give it him so hard that he'll hit the ground. And then—

And that's when Edmund hit his thumb with the hammer and started swearing and screaming blue murder. I never found out how he was going to continue exacting revenge on his father. I wondered what I would have done in his shoes … Would I have thought and felt the same way? I couldn't work it out.

So, I decided this was the sort of situation I didn't want to think about at all. One more. Cancer-Treblinka-Love-Fuck-Death …

And Edmund's dad.

I slotted him in between Fuck and Death. Preliminarily.

Even though it was hot, I liked sawing and nailing and building. Especially nailing. When you hammered nails, you seemed to be able to free yourself of all the things you didn't want to be thinking about. You could just concentrate on what you were doing. Bang. You just had to bang away. Drive the nail into the wood. Bang. Bang that bastard. Bang. Bang. Bang. And with an extra bang for good measure. When it couldn't go in any further.

Bang. To put it in its place. Now you're in there, you lousy nail, and that was the idea all along. No matter how hard you tried to be stiff and crooked and worm your way left and right. You shitty nail. Bang. I'm in charge here. Damn right. I thought of our carpentry teacher Gustav in school and about how there was woodwork and then there was woodwork.

The sun was still high when we were done. Henry inspected the eight-meter-long construction project, checking to see if the barrels were secured properly. He said he was going inside to make pancakes while we put the dock in place. "Okay?"

"Sure," said Edmund and we started to drag the fruit of our labor to the edge of the lake. Following Henry's drawing, we moored the dock with four ropes to two stable birches and anchored either end with a half-slack hawser. A bit of slack was essential, Henry had explained, but not too much. Then we stood and admired the wonder for a while before we slowly and with pride strode out over the planks. It was a little wobbly and in certain places your feet sank below the water line, at least when there were two of you, but, yes, it worked. We had built a goddamn dock.

Now we had a pontoon dock and twenty kronor. We looked at each other. Satisfaction.

"A brilliant summer," said Edmund with a tremble in his voice. "Hoo-hip, as they said in Ångermanland."

At the far end of the dock the water was nearly two meters deep and we managed to dive off thirty-eight times before Henry came out and shouted that the pancakes were ready. We ate as though we'd never seen food before and then went out and dived into the lake thirty-eight more times. We thought the sun might never set that night, so after Henry had made his diving debut and paid us each our promised ten kronor, we lay on the dock, reading or playing cards, which was tricky. You had to keep your ass in the wagon—as Edmund said in his Norrlandish way—otherwise the cards got wet.

But never mind. The point was that we were lying on planks we'd swiped and hammered together ourselves. And were floating on barrels we'd transported ourselves all the way from Laxman's and had expertly bound together. That was what this hot, neverending day was all about. Lying on your own dock.

"King of spades," said Edmund. "I hear a moped coming." I listened. Yes, the sharp noise of a moped zipping along was coming from the forest. It seemed to be just about in line with the Levis' place.

"Yes," I said. "Pass. A Puch, I think."

We played another few hands before we heard it stop and switch off up by the parking area. That made us lose our concentration. If we'd had any to lose in the first place.

"Eh," said Edmund. "I'm tired of this game. Let's call it a day."

"Works for me," I said, collecting the cards. I sat up on the dock with my legs in the water and looked toward the edge of the woods. Henry walked out onto the lawn. He had changed into jeans and a white nylon shirt.

I don't know if I had time to sense what was coming—anyway, afterward Edmund claimed he had—but about a minute after the moped's engine had been turned off up by the road, Ewa Kaludis appeared on Gennesaret's lawn. She was wearing a short white dress with a red shirt over it; when she spotted Henry she laughed and pulled a bottle of wine out of her tote bag—then she pressed herself against him and his white shirt.

Right then Edmund started to hiccup, an affliction that would last for several hours.

"No shit, hic," he said. "Your brother and Ewa Kaludis. Then it was them, hic, I heard ... no shit."

I got up. Wobbled and almost fell into the water but I caught myself. Made my way to the shore. Henry and Ewa Kaludis slowly turned toward me. Edmund hiccupped again. I felt paralyzed. Like I'd lost all sensation in my legs and so I had no choice but to stand on that patch of lawn for the rest of my life. In a dripping, faded bathing suit—oh well, it'd dry eventually—I swallowed and shut my eyes and counted to one, then Henry said:

"So, Erik, my brother. There's a lot I'm working on, like I said. A lot."

"Hi, Erik," Ewa Kaludis said. "And hello, Edmund."

"Hi, hic," Edmund said, behind me. He sounded like one of the frogs down by the lake. I opened my eyes and got my tongue and legs going again.

"Hi there, Miss Kaludis," I said. "I was just going to the john. See ya."

I sat there a while. Reading the same page of True Stories in an old issue of *Reader's Digest* fifty times. I don't know what was buzzing more—the three-quarter-full, summer-heated drum of shit beneath me or my fried noodle of a head—but I sat where I sat and it took a while. Only when Edmund knocked on the door and wondered if I'd had a shit-thrombosis—a rare illness from the depths of Medelpad—did I pull on my swimming shorts and give up. I opened the door and stepped out into the world.

"Hic," said Edmund and tried to smile like Paul Drake. "What do you think about this whole shebang? Berra Albertsson ... and everything."

"I don't know," I said.

"Some brother you have there," said Edmund cooly, but it was clear that he was more worried than he was letting on.

"He's out of his mind," I said.

"Hic," said Edmund. "You smell like shit."

Cancer-Treblinka ... I started to think, but I'd already forgotten where I'd put Edmund's father.

"Maybe we should just go for a swim?" I said.

"You don't have to ask me twice," said Edmund.

We swam until the sun had fully set and the mosquitoes started to buzz like crazy at the shoreline. Ewa Kaludis and Henry were on the dock, testing it out, and Ewa said that it seemed to be a sterling construction.

A sterling construction. I floated on my back out in the water and my entire body blushed. What would it be like at night?

"Exactly," said Edmund, splashing around like a goofy seal. "Built to last, hic. No more, no less."

Ewa Kaludis laughed.

"You're a funny one, Edmund," she said.

Then she linked arms with Henry and they went back to the house.

My brother Henry and Ewa Kaludis. She hadn't taken a swim, even though it had been so hot. Maybe she hadn't brought a swimsuit with her.

But she did try out the dock. Sterling work.

11

Before my mother got sick with cancer she said a number of strange things. It was in the weeks right before the diagnosis; maybe she sensed misfortune coming and wanted to impart some wisdom. A few words for the road before it was too late, I suppose.

"You're the dove, Erik," she'd say, looking at me with her mild, watery eyes. "Henry is the hawk; he always manages to come out on top. But you, you we have to look after, you're the one who has to watch his step."

These words came to mind when it started to sink in that Henry was involved with Ewa Kaludis. That he was actually *with* her. I mulled over this idea of the dove and the hawk and, thinking of Berra Albertsson, how lucky it was that Henry was a bird of prey. Because when Super-Berra found out what was going on between Ewa and my brother, well, there were sure to be consequences. I thought so, at least, but I knew what a miserable amateur I was when it came to navigating love's labyrinths.

And Edmund wasn't any better at it. Not one bit.

Love is like a train, I'd heard Benny's mom say. It comes and goes. Maybe there was something to it, but Benny's mother was probably no expert in matters of the heart either.

But I didn't really think much about it; it was hard to put words to, and to process. My brother and Ewa Kaludis. Kim Novak on the red Puch. Her breast against my shoulder in the classroom. Berra Albertsson and red-faced Mulle in Lacka Park.

That was more than enough already.

Anyway, we didn't hear much that night. Nothing that suggested they were in there, doing it at least. The tape deck was on low; Ewa laughed now and again: it had a sort of cooing sound. Henry's hoarse guffaw rose through the floorboards a few times. Nothing more. Maybe they were just sitting around talking, what did I know? Maybe that's what you did. When you weren't in the mood.

Still, Edmund and I stayed awake in the dark. We lay still in our beds, pretending to sleep, until we heard Ewa and Henry say goodbye out on the lawn. A minute passed and then the Puch fired up in the parking area. Edmund sighed deeply and turned toward the wall. I looked at my self-illuminating watch. It was two thirty; it had probably started to get light outside, but we had the blinds pulled down as usual.

Cancer-Treblinka-Love-Fuck-Death, I thought, somewhat dejected.

And Edmund's dad. And Henry and Ewa Kaludis. No, that was too heavy, as I said. Not worth thinking about.

It was nothing for a fragile dove to trouble his fried noodle with.

"It's a delicate situation. I take it you understand as much. Delicate."

From across the dining table, Henry gave us a serious look. First me, then Edmund. We looked back at him with equal gravity and each swallowed a bite of macaroni. It's much easier to look serious and inspire confidence when your trap isn't stuffed with macaroni. Especially if you happened to have mixed in too much flour, as Edmund had this time around.

"Of course," I said.

"Discretion is the better part of valor," said Edmund.

I had no idea what he meant, but that Edmund, he was full of strange expressions:

Discretion is the better part of valor.

Something is rotten in the state of Denmark.

Seh la gehr, *said the German.*

Not to mention all the Norrlandish.

"Good," said Henry. "I trust you. But remember: even if you think you know a lot, there's very little you understand."

"That doesn't just go for you. It goes for me too," he added after a while. "And for everyone else."

He waved his fork in the air in front of him, as if he wanted to write what he was saying in the void. "We'd be better off, us people, if we could keep ourselves from always having to create a damn context. We should give ourselves over to the fleeting present instead."

He fell silent and lit a Lucky Strike. Pensively blowing smoke across the dining table. It wasn't often that Henry let more than one sentence slip at a time, at least not with us, and the effort seemed to have tired him out.

"In the fleeting present," said Edmund. "I've always thought so."

"How's the book coming?" I interjected.

"What?" Henry said, staring at Edmund.

"The book," I said. "Your book."

Henry took his eyes off Edmund and took a drag.

"Can't complain," he said and stretched his arms over his head. "But you're not allowed to read it until you've turned twenty, remember that."

"Why not?"

"Because it's that kind of book," my brother said.

The hawk protecting the dove, I thought, and then that half-page popped into my head. The one I'd read eight or ten days ago, about the body that fell onto the gravel road, the dense summer night and all that. Suddenly I felt ashamed: as if without warning I had found myself in possession of something that was apparently forbidden and inappropriate for children. I don't know why. I muttered something in reply, but it seemed a response wasn't actually necessary, so I started shoveling more macaroni in my mouth.

"I was thinking about visiting Mom tomorrow," said Henry after he'd stubbed out his cigarette. "Want to tag along?"

I finished chewing. "No thanks," I said. "I don't think so. In a week or so, maybe."

"Your call," Henry said.

"Say hello for me," I said.

"Sure thing," Henry said.

"The soul lives right behind your vocal cords." That was another one of those strange things my mother said before she was admitted to hospital. "If you listen carefully, you'll always be able to tell the difference between right and wrong. Remember that, Erik."

The day after E-Day (E as in Ewa Kaludis) we rowed through the creek to get provisions from Laxman's, and I asked Edmund where he thought the soul lived in the body. And about right and wrong.

This seemed to be the first time Edmund had ever thought about it, because he missed a stroke and we glided right into the reeds. It was easily done: the creek seemed to be getting narrower and narrower with each passing day; the cabin owners usually got together and cleared it out once every summer, but it hadn't happened yet this year.

"Your mom has a handle on right and wrong," Edmund said once we were back on course. "Of course you know when you're doing something bad. When you're being mean to someone or ..."

"Or you've cleaned out a gum dispenser?" I said.

Edmund turned that over in his head.

"Chewing gum is one of the ills of youth, I'm sure of it. So, cleaning out a gum dispenser can never be completely wrong," he said.

"But it must be a little bit wrong?" I suggested. "Like stealing planks is."

"Darn little," said Edmund. "It's peanuts compared with ... well, if you compare it."

His sudden solemnity made me understand what he was comparing it to. Neither of us said anything for a while, but then he feathered the blades of the oars, placed them on the gunwales, and started to pat his body down.

"But where the soul lives, devil knows. It moves around. When I eat, it's in my stomach. When I read, it's in my head. When I think about Britt Laxman—"

"Enough," I interrupted. "I get it. You have a nomadic soul; that's probably because you've spent so much of your life moving around."

"Maybe," Edmund said, taking hold of the oars. "Have you told your brother about the fight in Lacka Park, how it went?"

"No," I said. "Why'd you ask?"

"Because my gypsy-soul tells me it's the right thing to do."

I was quiet for a bit.

"Henry always comes out on top," I said. "He's been to sea twice."

"Well, then," said Edmund. "I was just thinking. It's hot as hell."

"The long, hot summer," I said.

"That's one helluva song," Edmund said. "It can't hurt for us to keep our ears to the ground. About Henry and Ewa and what they're up to. What do you think?"

"White man speak with forked tongue," I said.

It was one of the best lines I knew. It could be used in any situation, except when you were talking to a native, and Edmund didn't have anything to add.

"No further questions," is all he said and continued rowing through the channel of reeds.

A few nights later I woke when Edmund sat up in his bed, gasping.

"What's the matter with you?" I asked.

"He must have picked her up in the car," said Edmund. "In Killer. I didn't hear a moped."

"What are you babbling about?"

"Listen," said Edmund and then I heard it, too.

Two distinct sounds.

One was Henry's bed creaking and groaning. Slow and steady. The other was Ewa Kaludis whining. Or moaning. Or gurgling. I didn't know which because I'd never heard a woman make noises like that before.

"My, my, my," whispered Edmund. "They're going at it so hard the whole house is shaking. I'm going to blow."

His jabbering upset me.

"Shut up, Edmund," I said. "You shouldn't talk like that about certain things."

Edmund fell silent. Leaving only the sound of Henry's

bed, rhythmically, insistently reverberating through the night. Throughout the house.

"Sorry," Edmund said after a while. "You're right, of course. But I'm going to sneak out and have peek anyway."

"Have a peek?" I asked.

"Sure," said Edmund. "We can spy on them from the stairs. They don't have a blind down there. It might be educational. Come on, don't dilly-dally."

For the first time in my fourteen-year-old life I had an erection so hard it hurt.

Edmund had probably thought we could each sit on a step and have a look, but that didn't work. The rickety stairs went up to our room along the gable wall, and across the top of the window in Henry's room. If we were going to see anything, god-willing, we'd have to stand in the flower bed near the wall with peonies, mignonettes, and a hundred different types of weeds. As stealthily as Indians, we sneaked there, and twice as stealthily as Indians we popped our heads up above the window ledge.

And then we saw everything.

It was like a movie, but there weren't any movies like that at that time, way back at the start of the sixties. But I had the vague notion that they'd exist in twenty years' time. Or thirty. Or a hundred; never mind, at some point there'd be films like this, if but for the simple reason that they were needed.

It was a vague notion. The rest wasn't vague at all.

Ewa Kaludis was straddling my brother. She was naked and her breasts were bouncing as she rose and sank over him. They were half-turned in our direction— well, she was, and that was the important part. They'd lit a few candles, which were stuck in empty bottles; every so often the flames flickered, and the light and shadow danced across her body.

Across her bare face and bare shoulders and bare breasts. Her slender, curvy, shining belly heaving and rolling and the glimpses of her dark sex, which was sometimes hidden by one of her thighs and Henry's hands.

I think both Edmund and I held our breath for five minutes.

Inside the dimly lit room Ewa Kaludis was making love to my brother; calmly and intently, it seemed; for a fraction of a second at a time we could see her whole sex and that he was in fact inside her, but it was enough. It was so beautiful. So goddamn beautiful I knew I'd never see such a sight again in my tiny, pathetic life. Never ever again. Even though my slim, erect fourteen-year-old dick ached like a broken bone, I started to cry. As softly and quietly as when we'd cycled through the summer night away from Lacka Park, I let the tears flow. Standing there in the weeds, staring and crying. Crying and staring. After a while I noticed that Edmund was jerking off. He'd started breathing with his mouth open, and his right hand shot up and down like a piston inside his pajama bottoms.

I took a deep breath and started to do the same.

Afterward, we crept away. Without a word, we walked over the dewy grass down to the lake. Wobbled out onto the pontoon dock and dived in as quietly as we could, so they wouldn't hear us back at the house. Pajama bottoms and all.

The water was as smooth as a mirror, warm and soft; I backstroked far, far out and floated on my back for a long while. Edmund had also swum out, but he kept his distance. It was clear we both needed space: two lonely fourteen-year-old boys in the middle of a summer night in a lake warmed by the July heat.

Edmund and I.

We hadn't exactly lost our virginities, but it was something like that. Something great and mysterious. I'd opened the door and witnessed something I'd been longing to see. Something that was like another country.

And it had been beautiful.

So goddamn beautiful. What else could we have done after that but go float in a lake?

Yes, that's what I remember thinking.

12

We were on our feet first thing the next morning even though we'd been awake for most of the night. Both Henry and Ewa were gone by the time we came down, so we assumed he'd given her a ride in the early hours of the morning. Of course she couldn't stay away for too long when visiting my brother.

Or so we assumed, so our fourteen-year-old brains reasoned. We didn't say much at all that morning. Edmund stirred his cereal around the soured milk for five minutes before he had a bite, as usual. He spread whey butter on his toast with ceremonious fuss. As if it were a task of grave importance, like a ground-breaking scientific experiment on which the future of mankind depended. As if spreading any over the crust or leaving a square centimeter unbuttered would cause the whole universe to explode.

I still remember searching for meaning in the difference between our ways of eating breakfast. Me, I usually polished off my toast and chocolate milk in under four minutes. For Edmund, breakfast was a kind of ritual, handled like a priest officiating at a communion service. Not that I had much experience of communion, but I had seen it once—when Henry was confirmed many years ago—and I'd never taken part in anything so slow or dull.

So maybe this difference in our breakfast rhythms meant something. Maybe it was one of those things that revealed the differences in our character, and if one of us had been female instead of male, it would have been impossible for us to live together as man and wife. Completely out of the question.

I had to smile at that last thought. I was only speculating to kill time while waiting for Edmund to finish up that morning. Loose, dumb speculation. Of course I'd never marry Edmund, however much of a woman I became, and I guess these thoughts appeared because I was tired of keeping my mind in check. That's what it was like inside my head those days. When I was alert and awake, all was well, but when I hadn't had enough sleep, anything could pop up. Cancer-Treblinka-Love ...

In any case, we had beautiful weather on this day too. We lay on the dock reading until mid-morning, and then we went out on the boat. We rowed to Fläskhällen first and played a few rounds on the new pinball machine. We didn't win a free turn; it was a stingy game on the whole and slightly tilted. When we'd had enough we ate ice cream and rowed out to Seagull Shit Island. We had a backpack full of apple juice, books, and *Colonel Darkin*. While Edmund tore through *Journey to the Centre of the Earth* for the fifth or sixth time, I tried my hand at some pretty involved panels. The image of Ewa Kaludis's breasts bouncing last night danced before my eyes, but however hard I tried, I couldn't capture it as it had been in real life. I couldn't even get close. So I decided that there would be no lovemaking depicted in *Colonel Darkin*. Not now, not ever. It wasn't my style, and it wasn't the Colonel's either.

When we'd taken our thirteenth dip and had opened the last apple juice, Edmund put on his glasses and said:

"I have a feeling."

It sounded serious and his expression was uncommonly earnest.

"You do?" I asked.

"Yes," Edmund said.

"What kind of feeling?"

Edmund hesitated.

"That it's all going to hell soon."

I took a gulp of juice and asked: "What's going to hell?"

Edmund sighed and said he didn't know. I waited before asking if maybe he meant what was going on between my brother and Ewa Kaludis. And Berra Albertsson.

Edmund nodded. "I think so," he said. "Something's gonna happen. It can't go on like this. It's like ... it's like waiting for a storm. Can't you feel it?"

I didn't answer. What my father had said that May evening at home in the kitchen on Idrottsgatan popped into my head.

A rough summer. It's going to be a rough summer.

Then I thought of Ewa Kaludis. And about Mulle, unconscious. About Edmund's real father. About my mother's gray hands resting on the hospital blanket. As somber as the color of blueberry-stained gruel.

"We'll see," I said in the end. "Only time will tell."

A couple of days passed. The heat held. We swam, lay on the dock and read, rowed to Laxman's and to Fläskhällen. Everything seemed back to normal. Henry sat in the shade, writing and smoking his Luckys, and we took care of the meals in exchange for fair compensation. Five or ten kronor. In the evenings Henry left in Killer and often didn't come home until late at night. He never said a word about Ewa Kaludis and neither did we ask. We bit our tongues and behaved like gentlemen. Like Arsène Lupin. Or the Scarlet Pimpernel.

Or Colonel Darkin.

"If you can't be anything else, you can damn well be a gentleman," went one of Edmund's sayings from Ångermanland, and I agreed with him—period.

The next time she appeared at Gennesaret, it was the fourth of July. I remember the date well because Edmund and I had been talking about George Washington and the Declaration of Independence. And about President Kennedy and his Jackie. It was a little past ten at night; we'd just had our chocolate milk and a buttered rusk, as we did before bedtime; it was a bright evening and Henry always had a cigarette lit to keep the mosquitoes away.

The three of us must have heard the moped at the same time. Edmund and I looked at each other across the kitchen table and the clatter of the typewriter stopped. It took her thirty seconds to reach the parking spot. She revved the engine and then switched it off.

"Hmm,'" said Edmund. "I need a whizz."

"Well, when you put it that way," I said.

At first I didn't recognize her. For one flashing second, I couldn't fathom that the woman who emerged from the lilacs and ran those few steps across the grass before throwing her arms around my brother was in fact Ewa Kaludis.

Ewa Kaludis/Kim Novak on the red Puch. Ewa Kaludis with the glittering eyes and the ripe, bouncing breasts. With the black slacks and the red hairband and the unbuttoned Swanson shirt fluttering in the wind.

But it was her. And she was wearing the Swanson shirt

and the slacks today too. Or a similar pair at least. But no red hairband. No glitter in her eyes and no broad smile. Just one eye, to be precise. The other, the right, looked like it had been replaced by two plums. Or like someone had smashed two plums where her eye was supposed to be. Her lips weren't themselves either. The upper lip had sort of been flattened and seemed to reach all the way up to her nose. The lower lip was large and swollen and had a wide dark line in the center. One of her cheeks bore a large bluish stain. She looked awful and it took me a moment to realize what must have happened. Somebody must've done this to her. Someone had used their fists on Ewa Kaludis's face. Someone had ... that someone ...

I think I blacked out as soon as I pieced it together. I hurt my eyes and heard Edmund cursing under his breath beside me. When I looked up, Ewa Kaludis was wrapped in my brother's embrace; he held her with both arms, stroking her back, and you could see that she was crying. Henry's head was bowed down, and he was mumbling something into her hair. Her shoulders shook in time with her sobs.

Other than Edmund letting out another trembling curse, nothing happened for a while. Henry helped Ewa sit down at the table where he'd been writing, and then he turned to us.

"Listen," he said, and his eyes darted between us. "I don't care what you do, but make damn well sure you leave us alone. Go to bed, or go rowing on the lake, anything, but Ewa and I have to be by ourselves now. Understood?"

I nodded. Edmund nodded.

"Good," said Henry. "Now, scram."

I cast a glance at Edmund. Then we went for a piss. Then we went to bed.

She was still there the next morning.

Edmund and I had discussed the situation for the better part of the night and we both slept until late morning. As I staggered down the stairs to get to the toilet before it was too late, Ewa was sitting on one of the chairs under the ash tree wearing Henry's ragged terry-cloth robe. She seemed to be freezing cold and when she hesitantly raised her hand in greeting, I got a lump in my throat. I had to swallow a few times to clear it.

"Hi," I said. "I'm just going to do my ablutions. I'll be back in a flash."

She did something with her face. Maybe she was trying to smile.

I peed, took a swim, and returned. Edmund was still snoozing. Henry was nowhere to be seen. I grabbed the other chair and sat down with Ewa. Across from her and to the side, quite close.

"Does it hurt?" I asked.

She shook her head gingerly.

"Not too bad."

I swallowed and tried not to look at her.

"It'll pass," I said. "In a few days you'll be the most beautiful person in the world again."

She tried smiling again, but had as much luck as with the last time. She flinched, presumably because of the pain, and put her hand in front of her mouth.

"I look terrible," she said. "Please don't look at me."

I turned my head away and studied the tree trunk instead. It was gray and rough and not particularly interesting.

"Where's Henry?" I asked.

"He went to town to buy some bandages. He'll be back soon."

"Okay."

After a long pause, I said: "It's terrible. I mean, that someone would do this to you."

She didn't reply. Just straightened up in the chair and cleared her throat a few times. I guessed she had blood in her throat. The victims in some of the books I'd read had that, and it sounded like she did, too.

"Can I get you anything?" I asked. "Something to drink?"

She blinked a few times with her good eye.

"No, thank you," she said. "You're sweet, Erik."

"Oh, bother," I said.

She cleared her throat again and wiped her forehead with the sleeve of the robe.

"You have to learn how to take it as it comes," she said. "You have to."

"Yeah?" I said.

"Don't worry about me. I've had worse."

"Worse?" I said.

"When I was your age," she continued. "And younger. I come from another country, as you may know. It was just me and my sister. My parents stayed behind. We traveled across the sea in a boat, not much bigger than your rowing boat ... I don't know why I'm telling you this."

"Neither do I," I admitted.

"Maybe it's because Henry told me about your mother," she said after a pause. "I know you're not having an easy time, Erik. I didn't know before, but I know now."

I nodded and looked at the pattern of the bark. It hadn't changed.

"You don't like talking about it?"

I didn't answer. Ewa studied me with her good eye. Then she leaned forward in the chair and patted the grass in front of her.

"Have a seat here, please."

I hesitated at first, but then I did as she said. I floundered out of the chair and sat on the ground between her knees. Rested my neck on the chair's slats. Felt her thighs on either side of me.

"Close your eyes," she said.

I closed my eyes. She took hold of my shoulders and gave me a slow, gentle massage.

Slow and gentle. Strong and warm. I felt dizzy. With all the new discoveries and experiences this summer, surely a hundred years must have passed since graduating from Stava School.

"Your shoulders are tense. Try to relax."

I relaxed and became like putty in her hands. I got an erection of course, but I made sure it was hidden in my baggy swimming trunks. Then I gave into the pleasure of sitting between Ewa's legs, enjoying her hands. I noticed I was crying again, but this time there weren't any tears. Just a pleasant, gentle buzz behind my eyes, and for one clear, bright second I knew what it was like to be Henry.

My brother Henry.

Eventually Edmund woke up, and eventually Henry returned from his trip to the pharmacy, but that didn't matter. When Ewa let go of my shoulders and mussed my hair it felt like we'd entered into a sworn fellowship. Or had made some sort of secret pact. We hadn't spoken much—not at all, actually. We were just sitting on the lawn together, but still it was something else, as Edmund might have said.

Well and truly something else. I thought about it once or twice a day in the time leading up to the Incident, and every time I did, a strong, hot feeling filled me. Hot and strong just like her hands on my tense shoulders.

The feeling of slipping into a nice hot bath after a cold winter's day, that's what I was thinking.

Like that, but radiating from within.

13

Henry left with Ewa that night. He must have rode the Puch and Ewa drove Killer; when you only have one good eye, it must be harder to drive a moped than it is to drive a car. In any case, the parking area was empty when Edmund and I returned around 10 p.m. from our long bike ride.

Then another couple of days passed. The weather volleyed between sun and rain. But overall it was nice and hot. We tried our hand at fishing, but Möckeln had a reputation for being dead when it came to fish, and anyway neither Edmund nor I were thrilled to be sitting around staring at a float.

Even less thrilled, in fact, by the thought of having to reel in a poor dace or perch and stick a knife in it. Or whack it until it died. Or whatever you did to fish.

As luck would have it, we never needed to come up with a solution to the problem because we didn't catch a single fish.

But Edmund did catch strep throat. A mild case—according to his own diagnosis; he'd had strep throat a few times before—but he was still lethargic and feverish and preferred to sleep. Or read.

"Read, sleep, drink," he said. "From these threads, my wellness is woven."

"Another saying from the heart of Lapland?" I asked.

"Not exactly," Edmund said. "My dad says that."

"Your real one?"

"No, for Christ's sake," said Edmund. "Not him. He's full of crap."

Those days it was harder than usual to talk to Henry. When he wasn't out with Killer running errands, he mostly went around muttering and smoking. His writing didn't seem to be moving forward either; often he just sat staring at the Facit, as if he were trying convince it to write the existential novel itself. Sometimes I heard him curse and tear a sheet of paper out of the roller. He was constantly grumbling and irate.

Because both my brother and Edmund were busy with themselves—Edmund with his strep throat, Henry with other things—I kept to myself as well. I drew more than ten pages of *Colonel Darkin and the Mysterious Heiress* and didn't think the result was too shabby. Since I'd decided to censor all the half-naked female bodies, it was much easier to get on with the story. I guess that's how it is, I thought with a measure of resignation. As in literature, so in life.

The monotony of those days carried over into mealtimes, too. Edmund had lost his appetite and when Henry ate, you got the feeling that you might just as well have set a plate of moss in front of him. He didn't care what he put in his mouth. Because of this and everything else, we mostly ate potatoes with butter. We put two jars of pickled herring on the table at every meal, but none of us bothered to twist off one of the lids and take a whiff.

It was what it was, and we had a decent stockpile of potatoes.

I'd just finished *And Then There Were None* and was facing the wall, about to fall asleep, when I heard them on the lawn.

Henry and Ewa. I looked at my self-illuminating watch. Twelve thirty. Edmund was breathing heavily with his mouth open over in his bed. It was a blustery day and every now and then a tree branch whipped the window. I couldn't help but think how safe and secure it felt lying in a warm bed. How free from danger.

Well, only for as long as you were lying in bed. The reality beyond the bed was another matter. Something else. The simple act of putting your feet on the cold floor and then going out into the world meant you were exposing yourself to countless risks and dangers. There were Henrys and Ewas and Edmunds, of course. But also black eyes and swollen lips and fists as hard and merciless as rock. Decisions to be made and matters to be handled whether you wanted to or not. Dads who hit and Treblinkas and cancerous tumors that grew and grew.

Out in the world. Beyond the bed, on the floor. I rolled over and pulled the blanket around me more tightly. I could hear Henry and Ewa speaking softly down below. No music tonight, apparently. No rhythmic creaking of the bed or lusty whimpers. It wasn't that kind of night. This night was different.

I wondered what they were talking about. I thought about that trick detectives used in the movies where they put a glass up against the wall. If that really did work, it could work with the floor as well.

There was a half-full glass next to Edmund's bed. Drinking plenty of liquids was part of his war against strep throat, so if I wanted to find out if I could hear them—if I really wanted to know what Ewa and Henry were discussing down there—it wouldn't have taken much. All I had to do was open the window and toss out the apple juice, lie on the floor with my ear to the glass, the glass to the wooden boards. Easy as pie.

I couldn't be bothered. Maybe I was too tired. Maybe I felt it wouldn't be gentlemanly.

If nothing else, you can damn well be a gentleman.

It wasn't a bad rule to live by, Edmund and I agreed. The gentility of standing in the flower bed and jerking to Ewa and Henry the other night was debatable, but surely even a gentleman had his off days. Like the sun has its spots.

I was musing from the comfort of my own bed. The voices below were but a distant mumbling and when I finally drifted off, my dream muted Henry's dark voice. I only heard Ewa's; she was speaking to me. She was sitting next to me in bed, or rather, behind me and to the side, and she was massaging my tense shoulders again.

My shoulders and other things. If I'd never woken up from that dream, it wouldn't have mattered.

The next morning, there was a note on the kitchen table that read: *Have a lot to take care of. Will be back after midnight. Meatballs and peaches in the pantry. Henry.*

It wasn't like my brother to leave a note about what he was up to, and I guessed Ewa Kaludis was behind it. Henry wasn't usually away from Gennesaret for more than six or eight hours at a time and now he'd be gone both day and night, apparently, but it still wasn't like him to leave a note like this. Not my brother.

I checked to see if there really were two cans on the shelf in the pantry. There were. One with Mother Elna's moose meatballs in a creamy sauce. One with halved pears in thick syrup. It didn't sound half bad, even if I didn't really see the point of the syrup. Assuming

Edmund's lack of appetite held strong, I could—if nothing else—look forward to one square meal later in the day. Shame there wasn't any cream for the peaches, but biking or rowing all the way to Laxman's for a splash of cream seemed excessive. Not worth worrying about with the clouds of unease that had been rolling in lately.

It was quite an idle day. At least to begin with. Edmund was on the mend, he said, but only slightly. It would probably take another day or two to be rid of the damn strep, he figured.

So: sleep, read, and drink, then. No outings whatsoever. Not to Laxman's, not anywhere. There were no two ways about it, he had no desire to get out of bed. He was "convalescing," as they liked to say in Västerbotten.

I placed two bottles of apple juice on the table, wished him well, and went outside and sat on one of the easy chairs with *Darkin* and a new Agatha Christie. The last one hadn't been bad; the new one was called *The Murder of Roger Ackroyd* and Edmund said it was one hell of a story.

And that was basically how I spent the day before the Incident. Sitting in the sun lounger with *Colonel Darkin* and Agatha Christie. Edmund came out a few times, but when the sun was shining he thought it was too hot and when it disappeared behind the clouds, he froze. He complained he was having a hard time reading, because he kept forgetting what was on the pages he read at bedtime and had to start from the top when he woke up. I suggested he try rereading *Journey to the Center of the Earth*—you could make sense of that one backward and upside-down—but he said he wasn't in the mood for Jules Verne. He needed something like Patrick Quentin and Ellery Queen, and you couldn't really read crime novels more than once.

There were exceptions, of course.

I prepared the moose meatballs in the middle of the afternoon. I ate nine; Edmund ate one. We split the peaches between us more evenly, four–two. All in all, I was satisfied with my meal.

Even though I had to cook *and* do the dishes.

Just as I'd finished with the latter, we received our first caller of the afternoon. Gladys Lundin walked across the property clearing her throat and coughing, asking if we had any schnapps to spare.

Normal people, like Benny's mom or Mrs. Lundmark, who lived two floors up on Idrottsgatan, would knock and ask for a cup of sugar or flour for pancakes or rhubarb pie, but the Lundins were not normal people. Far from it. As far as I knew, Gladys was the matriarch of the tribe; she was at least seventy and probably weighed well over one hundred kilos. She propelled herself forward with two sturdy oak canes and always had a lit cigarette dangling from the corner of her mouth. None of this prevented her from stopping by to beg for schnapps.

I explained that the house was dry for the time being, and so she asked for a kilo of potatoes instead.

I could hardly deny her that, after all we had half a crate. With the canes and the cigarettes, the carrying became complicated, but in the end I hung a bowl on a cord around her neck. She hobbled away without saying thank you and I wondered if she was going to sit right down and brew some schnapps with the potatoes as soon as she got home. I only had a vague idea of how that would go, but with some luck she might distill a glass by the evening.

From that day onward, I thought it was strange that one person showed up right after the other—Gladys Lundin and the next visitor—however, whichever way I looked at it, I couldn't make a logical connection.

But never mind; after getting rid of Gladys I hadn't been in the chair for more than twenty minutes before I heard another cough behind me. Much stronger and much more ominous.

I stood up and found myself eye-to-eye with Bertil Albertsson. Super-Berra. The man who had an arm so strong that if a ball he threw hit a goalie, it could be fatal. The man who had hung his striped blazer nonchalantly on one finger and handed it to Atle Eriksson before he let rip on red-faced Mulle in Lacka Park.

The man whose fiancée was called Ewa Kaludis.

I'd dropped *Colonel Darkin* on the lawn, but I didn't think to pick it up. I had a hard time swallowing and wondered if Edmund had given me his strep throat. Berra was standing before me with the same wide stance that he'd had at Lacka Park. He was wearing a white, short-sleeved shirt and his tanned, hairy arms were rippled with muscles and veins. His rough-hewn face was inscrutable; he had one eyebrow cocked, and looked at me like something he happened to have stepped on in the gutter.

"Hi," I said.

He didn't reply. His one eyebrow stayed raised, almost up to his hairline, and his jaw was moving slightly. Grinding. I couldn't think of anything to say, so I tried to stare right back at him. No use.

"Where's your brother?" he said. Without moving his lips.

"Who?" I asked.

How did I come up with such an utterly stupid question? I was probably trying to buy some time. Time to faint, or time for some merciful god or goddess to come to my rescue. To arrive at Gennesaret and carry me off to a desert island in the South Seas for all eternity.

No god appeared and I didn't faint.

"Your brother," Berra Albertsson repeated. "Henry. I've got a thing or two to say to him."

"Oh, him," I said.

"How many brothers do you have?" asked Berra.

"Just one," I said.

"So where is he?"

"He's not here," I said.

"When will he be back?"

"I don't know. Late."

"Late?"

"Tonight. Twelve. Or even later. He left a note."

"Tonight."

"Yes."

"Hmm." He lowered his eyebrow, coughed twice, and spat on the lawn. The loogie landed twenty centimeters from my left foot. Five centimeters from *Colonel Darkin*.

"You tell him," he said. "Tell him I'll be back at one tonight. I've got a thing or two to say to him."

"He might not be here then, either," I said. "He might be even later."

"So I'll wait."

And with that he left. I watched him go. When he'd disappeared behind the lilac bushes, I looked down at the spit shimmering in the grass.

It's never going to go away, I thought. That damned loogie is going to be on Gennesaret's lawn a century from now. It is what it is.

"Who were you talking to?" Edmund asked, sticking his head out of the window. "I was sleeping and heard voices. Who was here?"

Edmund went as pale as a corpse when I told him about my conversation with Berra Albertsson.

He took his glasses off and put them back on again at least ten times and gnashed his teeth, but mostly he looked frightened. Dogged and focused in spite of the fever, but also despairing. This must have been what it was like when he was waiting for his real dad to belt him. He barely said a word as I recounted my conversation with Berra. He wrung his hands every now and then and struggled to swallow, but that was all. He had no idea what we should do.

Not a single one.

"The storm," he finally said. "I told you. We've been waiting for the storm and now it's here."

"Goddammit," I said, because I didn't know what to say and I felt the need to buck myself up with a few swear words. "Damn it all to hell."

"Exactly," said Edmund.

The rain started to fall around 8 p.m. and I kept Edmund company by going to bed just after nine. It was a proper storm with streaks of lightning and thunder claps too close for comfort. It seemed like it would never end.

"Some storms go round and round," Edmund said. "In Ånger once the thunder and lightning went on for over twelve damn hours in a row. Talk about something that can make you feel real small."

"How's the strep?" I asked, because I didn't want to talk about storms. It was bad enough as it was.

"On the mend, I'm sure," Edmund concluded after swallowing a few times to see. "I'll probably be all better by tomorrow."

Ten minutes later he was sleeping like a log. I turned off the light and lay awake listening to the rain on the roof and the rumbling. The lightning was striking fifteen or thirty seconds before the bangs, so maybe it was like Edmund said: the storm was circling us.

And it did make you feel real small.

I must have fallen asleep, because soon after twelve I woke up. The rain had stopped but there was a spirited wind.

I heard Henry turn on the tape deck downstairs. I think he was talking to someone.

Edmund's bed was empty.

II

14

It was Lasse Side-Smile who found the body, and it was Lasse Side-Smile who landed on the front page of *Kurren* two days in a row. His parents had a cottage in Sjölycke and that's where Side-Smile spent most of the summer. It was a well-known fact that he was realizing his dream of becoming a competitive cyclist. Like Harry Snell. Or Ove Adamsson. His face ruled out any chance of him becoming a film star or a trumpet player, but nothing was keeping him from being a speed-demon.

He had been in the town's junior league for a few seasons and was expected to move up to the seniors in a year or so. A up-and-comer, as they say in sports. Side-Smile had all the prerequisites—everyone who knew anything about cycling agreed—and his face was no obstacle.

Given his ambition, Side-Smile took advantage of the summer days for training, and in the small hours of the morning he would take his racing bike out of the shed in Sjölycke and hit the road for a fifty- to sixty-kilometer ride. Or eighty to one hundred if he was on top form— and this was one of those days. Riding the uneven gravel roads wasn't usually part of his routine because there was a clear and present risk of skidding and flat tires.

But that morning he did. For variety's sake, I suppose, and there was still the odd race track on gravel at this time, the dawn of the sixties.

He took the road that led east through the woods, toward the Levis' place, and it turned out to be an especially short spin.

Short and one hell of a shocker, as he later told the reporter from *Kurren*. Only a few kilometers into the ride, he comes charging down the winding road that led past the parking area we shared with the Lundins. At full speed. Hunched over the handlebars. Sees two parked vehicles. A black vw and a red Volvo pv 1800.

The Volvo makes him hit the brakes so hard he almost lands on his nose in the gravel.

Or rather, what's next to the Volvo does.

The passenger's door is open and just below it on the ground is a person lying on their stomach. A man wearing narrow black shoes, thin polyester slacks, and a white short-sleeved shirt. This is what Side-Smile sees when he turns his bike around and backtracks up the hill. He glimpses a striped blazer on the driver's seat. The man is on his front, but slightly contorted, arms alongside his body. As Side-Smile keeps repeating to the reporters and the photographers: The arms were what made it click.

Something wasn't right.

A person who's alive doesn't lie like that. You can tell at a glance, at least if you have a pair of eyes in your head, and Side-Smile certainly does. It's about quarter past six and he's guiding his racer toward this unbelievable sight with great caution.

He sees what he already knows.

The man has a gaping hole in his head, and everything is covered in blood: his hair, his shirt, and the ground on which he lies.

He can't tell who it is, because of course he doesn't dare touch the body and turn it over. You're not supposed to do that, anyway. It's the police's job to turn dead bodies over, not Lasse Side-Smile's.

No, Side-Smile doesn't identify the man in the clearing; we do. Henry and Edmund and I, because we're the ones he comes running to, shouting at the top of his lungs.

And it's we who run with him up the path, and we who stand in a semi-circle around Bertil "Berra" Albertsson, and not one of us says a word.

Not a single one of us. All three of us know it's Super-Berra, but none of us lets anything slip. Not one sound.

Neither does Lasse Side-Smile. For a full thirty seconds, four people just stand there, staring at a fifth who is no longer a person, and these are the longest thirty seconds of our lives.

Then I check my watch. It's six twenty-five the morning of July tenth and the Incident is a fact.

When Lasse Side-Smile left to go call the police from the Lundins', I knew there was something I had to find out, even though my head felt scrambled. I managed to make eye contact with my brother Henry and to mouth the question "Ewa?," looking in the direction of Gennesaret. I don't know why I felt like keeping Edmund out of it, but I did. This was between me and my brother. This, whatever it was.

I think Henry understood me, but he didn't answer. He gave his head a slight shake and lit a Lucky Strike.

I sighed and put my arm around Edmund. He was shivering in the cold morning air, but otherwise, it was just as he'd predicted.

The strep throat had eased during the night.

15

The first police car arrived while we were still by the parking spot. Side-Smile had returned—along with Gladys Lundin and a lady about thirty years her junior who was a carbon copy of her. Smaller and paler, she didn't have a cane yet, but she was valiantly chain-smoking and her breasts were already drooping down toward her belly button.

"That's how that cookie crumbled," was Gladys's first comment. "Lucky none of the men are home, or the cops would march right over and pick them up."

Otherwise, there weren't many comments floating around. Super-Berra was where he was on the gravel, but no one seemed to want to take a closer look. We spread out in a protective semi-circle of sorts, with our backs turned to the Incident, and when the black-and-white Amazon turned up with one plain-clothes and three uniformed policemen, we had to give them our names and then trudge home and sit tight.

"Goddamn," said Edmund when we were back in our room. "That's all I can say. Goddamn."

I realized I was feeling properly sick and considered going into the woods and sticking a finger down my throat, but the waves of nausea retreated. I shut my eyes and hoped for a couple hours' sleep, but that was wishful thinking. From the ground floor, I heard Henry on the Facit; it was strange that he'd be writing at a time like this, and indeed the clatter stopped after a few minutes.

"Hey, Erik," said Edmund.

"Yes?" I said.

"Let's not talk about it now. I can't hack it."

"All right," I said. "Best we get some shut-eye first."

"He's dead," Edmund said anyway. "Can you believe the bastard is dead?"

"Yes," I said. "Berra Albertsson is dead."

The detective arrived around nine and was called Lindström. He was wearing a pale suit and a bow tie, and, if it wasn't for his black, slicked-back hair, he might have looked like Tam Sventon, Private Detective.

One by one, he greeted us, by shaking our hands and telling each of us his name, Detective Superintendent Verner Lindström. He smelled faintly of cologne and spoke slowly and thoughtfully, as if he were making an effort to discard any unnecessary and frivolous words before saying what he wanted to say. He exuded a certain confidence, and I could tell he wasn't to be toyed with.

Naturally, he started with Henry. They locked themselves away in the kitchen and as Edmund and I wandered around the house we could see them sitting in there at the table covered with the checked wax cloth, almost like two chess players.

Because we didn't really know what to do with ourselves, we went up to the clearing to have a look.

Four other cars had arrived at the scene; it had been roped off and the black-and-yellow signs announced that a crime scene investigation was under way and it was forbidden for unauthorized persons to cross the police line. Edmund explained to a cocky constable that we were the ones who'd found the body—well, not counting Lasse Side-Smile—but that didn't help. We had no business being there. Berra Albertsson's body had been removed and thick chalk lines had been traced around where it had lain.

Several men in green overalls were crawling in and around the red Volvo. They wore thin gloves, had brushes and magnifying glasses. Suddenly, the scene felt so unreal I had to pinch myself in the arm to make sure I wasn't dreaming. Edmund noticed what I was doing and shook his head gravely.

"It won't help," he stated. "Just accept you're awake, pal."

People were milling around outside the barrier, but not a lot. I saw Side-Smile and his dad, the old Levi couple and a few folks from the Sjölycke area. As well as a couple of journalists and a photographer.

But not a lot, as I said. The world probably didn't yet know that the handball legend Berra Albertsson was dead. You could almost still tell yourself nothing had happened.

This feeling didn't last long. The next thing I noticed was that Killer was inside the police line and that for some reason it gave me the shivers.

Yes, I must've been awake this whole time.

When we arrived back at Gennesaret, Henry's interrogation was finished. It was Edmund's and my turn to sit at the kitchen table with Detective Lindström. Before we went inside I thought about when Berra and I had talked out on the lawn not twenty-four hours ago.

"I'm just going to check on something," I said to Edmund and left him for a few seconds.

Of course. There wasn't even a trace of the loogie left.

"As you know, there has been a serious incident," the detective began. "It's important that everyone's statement is as accurate as possible so that we can sort this out. No guessing. No lies. Is that clear?"

Edmund and I nodded.

"Your names, please."

We gave them.

"And you're living here this summer?"

"Yes," I said.

"Together with Henry Wassman, who is also your brother?"

"Yes."

"What time did you go to bed last night?"

Edmund explained that he had gone to bed at eight thirty on account of his strep throat. I said I was in bed about half an hour later.

Detective Lindström didn't have a tape recorder, but using a blue ballpoint pen he wrote down every word we said in a notepad that was in front of him on the table. He kept one arm bent around the pad, so it was impossible to read his writing. You could tell it wasn't his first time questioning someone, and my respect for him grew.

"And what time did you fall asleep, approximately?"

"At once," explained Edmund.

I hesitated. "Ten, I think."

"Was either of you awake later in the night?"

Edmund wrinkled his forehead and I let him answer first.

"I went out for a pee," he said.

"At what time?"

"No idea," said Edmund. "Not a clue."

"And you didn't notice anything unusual at that time?"

"No," said Edmund. "Nothing."

"Was it raining?"

Edmund thought about it.

"No," he said. "It wasn't raining."

Detective Lindström made a note.

"And you?" he said, turning to me. "Were you awake at any point during the night?"

"No," I said. "I don't think so."

"Not at all?"

"No."

"Was your brother at home last night?"

"No."

"What time did he come home?"

"I don't know. Not while I was awake, in any case."

He turned back to Edmund.

"Did you notice if Henry was home when you were relieving yourself?"

"No idea," said Edmund.

"You didn't see if his light was on?"

"I think it was off. Why don't you ask Henry when he came home yourself, Detective Lindström, sir?"

Lindström didn't bother to answer. Instead, he trained his eyes on me.

"And there's nothing else you think we should know about?"

"No."

He wrote a few words on the pad.

"Tell me what happened this morning," he said.

Edmund and I took turns retelling how Lasse Side-Smile's shouts from down on the lawn had woken us. How, together with him and Henry, we'd rushed up to the parking area to see what had happened. How we'd waited there while Side-Smile called the police from the Lundins'.

"Do you know who was on the ground?" Lindström asked.

Edmund and I looked at each other.

"Yes," I said. "It was Berra Albertsson."

Lindström nodded.

"You knew that already then? As soon as you saw him."

"Yes."

"How come you recognized him?"

"We'd seen him before," said Edmund.

"Where?" said Lindström.

"Around," said Edmund. "In Lacka Park."

"He's been in the papers, too," I added. "In *Kurren*."

Lindström adjusted his bow tie and made a note. Leaned back and thought for a few seconds.

"Did he pay you a visit?"

"Berra Albertsson?" said Edmund. "No, he didn't."

"Never," I said. "Not while I've been home, at least."

"Do you know if your brother was acquainted with him?"

"No," I said. "I'm sure he wasn't."

"Have you seen him around? In Sjölycke or anywhere around Möckeln?"

We thought about it.

"No," said Edmund.

"No," I said.

Lindström took a tube of Bronzol out of his inner pocket and shook out two pastilles. Weighed them in his hand and then tossed them in his mouth with a practiced gesture.

"Are you sure? Are you sure you've never seen Berra Albertsson in the area?"

"Absolutely," said Edmund.

"Only in Lacka Park," I said.

"And you didn't hear anything unusual last night?"

We shook our heads. Detective Lindström chewed on the Bronzol pastilles, deep in thought.

"All right then," he said, and with that the interrogation was over.

Our fathers took the twelve o'clock bus and Laxman picked them up in Åsbro in his yellow taxi.

"You can't stay here," said my father.

"It's out of the question," said Edmund's dad.

"Take it easy," said Henry.

Edmund's dad took out a handkerchief that was as big as a tent and patted his face and neck.

"Easy?" he snorted. "How the heck can we take it easy? A murder was committed one hundred meters from here. Are you nuts?"

Edmund's dad looked at Henry, eyes wide, and when Henry didn't answer he turned to my father. "Is he nuts?"

"You have to go back to town," my father repeated. "This won't work. It's unbelievable. Nothing like this has ever happened before."

Henry lit a Lucky Strike and got up from the kitchen table.

"Do what you like with the boys," he retorted. "But I'm staying here."

"You want to go home, right, boys?" Edmund's dad asked, using a milder tone. "You do want to get back to town as soon as possible?"

I looked at Edmund. Edmund looked at me.

"Not on your life," said Edmund.

"Unbelievable," my father repeated. "I'm speechless."

"Don't you understand? A murderer is on the loose!" said Mr. Wester.

They stayed the whole day and spent the night, and the next day Edmund and I agreed to go back to town with them if they promised we could return to Gennesaret the day after, as long as no other act of violence was committed around Möckeln. Edmund went home, and I went with my father to the hospital and sat for an hour with my mother. Her hair had been washed and set in permanent waves, but otherwise she seemed about the same as before. Maybe she was paler. We spoke about Berra Albertsson's murder the entire time—the newspapers had dedicated several pages to it—or, more precisely, my mother and father talked about it while I mostly sat there, nodding and pretending to agree with everything they said. The results from the doctors' latest tests weren't ready yet, so there wasn't really much else to discuss. It was what it was.

Before we left the hospital my mother clasped my hand between both of hers for a while. She looked at me with a kind of gravity and I thought she might share another one of her strange words of wisdom.

She didn't.

"Take care of yourself, my boy," is all she said. "Take care of yourself and take care of Edmund, too."

We went home on the eight o'clock bus. Then I slept one night at Idrottsgatan and the next day, a Saturday, Henry came and picked Edmund and me up and we went back to Gennesaret.

16

Even though we were so close to the heart of the action, we found out about the police's progress with the case in the *Kurren* and *Läns* newspapers along with everyone else. On the first day, Police Chief Elmestrand explained that there was a good chance of finding the perpetrator in the near future, and they had no intention of calling in the National Criminal Investigation Department. He had total faith in Detective Lindström and his men, he said, but welcomed any and all tips from the Great Detective Public. It was important that everyone did their part to help solve this brutal crime, this tragedy that had befallen our district and the Swedish sporting community.

The national handball team had been dealt a blow to the solar plexus, as a journalist called Bejman put it in *Läns*.

As far as the suspect's identity was concerned, by Saturday the police still didn't have any answers. They said they had several leads, but it was too soon to direct their suspicions at any one person.

Perhaps it was the work of a madman. Perhaps there were ulterior motives.

According to the reported facts in the papers, it was

assumed that Bertil "Berra" Albertsson had met his killer sometime between twelve and two on the night between Wednesday and Thursday. Apparently, the perpetrator had launched his attack just as Albertsson was getting out of his car in the small parking lot where he was later found—next to the gravel road that ran through the forest between Sjölycke's recreational area and the Fläskhällen beach on Lake Möckeln. They were still in the dark about what Albertsson had been doing there at that time of day. In spite of the information provided by people who had known the deceased—his fiancée Ewa Kaludis, for instance—nothing had surfaced that could shed light on the matter.

The murder itself had been committed with a so-called blunt object, probably a heavy hammer or a small sledgehammer. A single blow was all it took; contact was made with Albertsson's head from above, cracking through the crown of his skull, deep into his brain. It was assumed that death was instantaneous.

"Right in the noggin," said Edmund as he set *Kurren* aside. "How about a swim?"

From the start, Edmund and I seemed to have an understanding. An unspoken understanding that we wouldn't talk about the murder. Not more than was absolutely necessary. But of course neither of us could stop thinking about it; it overshadowed everything else. The Incident worked its way into every nook and cranny of our minds, and so, to talk about it on top of that would just have been too much.

Far too much. That went without saying.

Edmund and I had a lot of these unspoken understandings. While it felt completely natural, it was also strange. We hadn't spent more than a couple of months together, and yet we knew where we stood with each other. It was as if we had known each other our entire lives. I remember thinking once that we could have been twins.

But this didn't apply to Ewa Kaludis. We had to put her on the agenda every so often, that was clear.

"I wonder," Edmund said. "I wonder what she said to the police about her black eye?"

"She's probably not feeling too good right now," I said.

"Must be lonely," said Edmund. "Without Henry and all that. You don't think they're seeing each other?"

"As far as that goes, I don't think anything about anything," I said.

The idea of looking her up had already sprouted in the back of my mind. In Edmund's, too, apparently.

On Sunday, Detective Lindström returned. He didn't stay more than an hour, but he spoke with all three of us. One after the other, and this time to me and Edmund separately.

"I'm here to go over a couple of details," he explained when it was my turn.

"Details?" I said.

"Details," said Lindström. "They might seem insignificant, but the picture always comes together through the details."

"Only time will tell," I said.

He furrowed his brow for a moment. Then he turned a page in his notebook and clicked his pen a few times.

"You got a lot of tools out here?"

"Tools?"

"Saws, axes, hammers and so on."

"Well," I said. "Some, not many."

"We're mainly interested in a large hammer or a small sledgehammer."

"I see."

"Do you know if you have one of those."

I thought about it.

"There's a hammer in the tool box," I said. "But it's not that big."

"This one?"

He held up a hammer that he'd been hiding under the table. I made a quick assessment.

"Yes."

"Are you sure?"

I looked at it more closely. "Yes, that's the one. We used it when we built the dock; I recognize it."

"Good," said Lindström. "Matches up with what your friend said."

I didn't say anything.

"What about a bigger one?"

"Yeah, there is," I said. "I think there's a small sledge-hammer or something out in the shed."

"Is there?" said Lindström. "Let's take a look."

I followed him out to the tumbledown shed next to the outhouse. Unlatched the door and looked in at the mess.

"I don't really know where it is."

I poked around.

"Can't you find it?" Lindström wondered. He had taken out his tube of Bronzol and was rocking from heel to toe.

"Don't seem to be able to."

"It doesn't matter. I don't think it's here. Your brother couldn't find it either. You don't happen to know where it might have gone?"

I stepped out of the shed and brushed off the dust.

"No," I said. "I really don't."

"Do you remember when you saw it last?"

I shrugged.

"Dunno. A few weeks ago, maybe."

"You didn't use it when you were building the dock?"

"No."

We went back to the kitchen table.

"The other detail," Lindström said after writing in his notepad. "The other detail concerns one Miss Ewa Kaludis."

"Oh?"

"Are you acquainted with her?"

"She was a substitute teacher at school," I said. "In May and June. But only for a few subjects. Our usual teacher had broken her leg."

Lindström nodded.

"Was she a good teacher?"

"Ah, yes. I guess she was."

"Did you know she kept company with Berra Albertsson?"

"Yes."

"Have you seen her at all this summer?"

"No," I said. "Oh wait, yes. Once in Lacka Park."

"Lacka Park?"

"Yes."

"Only there?"

"Yes."

"Not on any other occasion?"

"No."

"Are you sure?"

I thought about it.

"Not that I remember," I said.

Lindström was silent for a few seconds but didn't make any notes. Then he stood up.

"I might be stopping by again," he said. "If you find that sledgehammer, get in touch."

"I will," I promised.

We shook hands and then he was on his way.

Once in fourth grade Balthazar Lindblom wet himself. It happened during religious education with a substitute teacher called Rockgård, whom we called Rockhard, because he was. He was incorruptible. It was no use trying to be cheeky or doing things differently from how he'd decided.

Balthazar's accident happened with about ten minutes of the lesson to go, and because we were silently working from our textbooks, everyone noticed the gushing sound coming from under his desk.

Even Rockhard.

"What in all—" he barked. "What is going on, you ninny?"

Balthazar finished peeing before answering. The puddle kept spreading, and those of us who were sitting near him had to lift our feet off the ground.

"Teacher said so," Balthazar said.

"What?" Rockhard asked. "What do you mean?"

"Teacher said we had to make sure to visit the toilet during breaktime. That there was no point in asking to go during the lesson."

It was probably the only time in his teaching career that Rockhard ended his class ten minutes before the bell.

And Balthazar Lindblom is the only person I know who managed to become some sort of hero—if only for a short time—just by wetting his pants.

As time passed, it wasn't so much the peeing as Rockhard's response that stuck in my mind. What he said before he ushered us out into the playground, that is.

"Perfect. You handled this perfectly, my boy."

I thought of Rockhard when Detective Superintendent Lindström left Gennesaret that Sunday afternoon. Not because they were especially alike, neither in their manner nor in their looks, but because they had something in common. Something incorruptible. Something there was no use in trying to influence or oppose.

Was this for better or worse? Who knows.

To be honest, it was the first time that summer Britt Laxman paid Edmund and me any attention. That Monday morning, I mean, when we walked under the ringing bell into the shop in Åsbro.

The first and only time, actually.

"Well, hello there," she said. Flashing her teeth and losing interest in the gray-haired woman at the counter airing her complaints. "Hi Erik. Hi, Edmund. How's it going?"

At least she'd learned our names. I looked at Edmund and around the shop. It was unusually crowded. I could tell Britt Laxman wasn't the only one who knew who we were. I could tell most of them weren't there just to go shopping. The sudden silence and tongue-tiedness were connected to our arrival, that was crystal clear. On the one hand it was flattering, but it was also threatening, and I'm pretty sure Edmund felt the same.

Three seconds, no longer than that, but it was long enough. We looked at each other knowingly. Old Major Casselmiolke cleared his throat and continued the train of thought he'd begun with Moppe Nilsson at the meat counter.

"Tracks!" thundered the military man. "There have to be tracks! Clues, for heaven's sake! They're just waiting for the analysis! We live in a scientific age, don't you forget that!"

"Allow me to disagree," Moppe countered leisurely while moving the sausages around with his sausage-like fingers. "The perpetrator should be thanking God for the rain."

"The rain?" said Casselmiolke. "God?"

As if he'd never heard of such things.

"The rain that fell between four and five in the morning," Moppe explained. "It would have washed away every last clue. That's what it said in *Aftonbladet* this Saturday."

"*Aftonbladet*?" said Casselmiolke. "I've never touched that rag! You don't happen to have a copy to spare, do you?"

"I'm sorry, no," Britt Laxman called from across the store. "They sold out in half an hour." Then she turned to us wide-eyed and with a fresh smile. "What'll it be?" she asked. "And how are you both doing?"

We went through the shopping list as quickly as we could, but when we were done, she didn't want to let us go.

"What do you think?" she lowered her voice—so at least not every last person in the shop could hear her. "Who did it?"

Edmund glanced at me.

"A madman," he then said. "Some nut-job who escaped from a loony bin. Isn't that obvious?"

And that was the line we continued to toe. The madman line. When people asked us what we thought, which God knows they did—after all we'd seen the body, we lived right by the scene of the crime, we must've heard something in the night, and so on—we went with the lunatic theory. A madman. An escaped mental patient. Only someone who was out of his mind could've been behind the murder of Bertil "Berra" Albertsson. Of course. Anything else was unthinkable.

We knew in an instant—as soon as we were out on Laxman's steps, and without having to discuss it—that this had been exactly the right response.

A madman.

Who else?

17

During those nights, I started dreaming about Ewa Kaludis again. Sometimes she had a black eye, sometimes not. I suspected Edmund was dreaming of her in his bed, too, and when I asked, he admitted it freely.

"Of course," he said. "She's got her hooks in mc. Britt Laxman feels sort of stale now."

"Britt Laxman? You're not saying you used to dream about her?"

"Well," said Edmund. "Not dream, exactly. Fantasize."

Soon we were talking about whether or not it was possible for two people to dream the same dream. Could Edmund and I, each in our own bed, be looking at the same images of Ewa Kaludis? Like sitting in the cinema and watching the same film?

I didn't see why not. The dream factory might have some sort of rationing program and there might just not be enough unique dreams to go around for each person each night.

Edmund disagreed.

"They can't be that darn stingy in the dream world," he said. "It's only in our crap world that you have to go around scrimping and scrounging. Can't we at least have our dreams to ourselves?"

To each person a dream?

I hoped Edmund was right. It sounded fair and democratic—as Brylle would say during social studies. As for our nightmares, we never discussed those.

After the murder my brother Henry stuck closer to Gennesaret than before, but that didn't make him any more talkative. He didn't write much either; mostly he lay on his bed, reading what he'd already written, I think. He took Killer out for short spins and went for a row on the lake a few times too. But he was rarely gone for more than an hour. On Tuesday morning, he said he had to go to Örebro and would be away for a while. He set off soon after twelve, and Edmund and I decided to give the pinball machine down at Fläskhällen another try. We were just about to set off in the boat when a man appeared around the side of the house.

He looked to be in his thirties. But with thinning hair. He wore a white nylon shirt and sunglasses and was waving both of his arms, so we'd understand that he wanted to have a word with us.

We looked at each other and went ashore.

"Lundberg," he said when we'd reached him. "Rogga Lundberg. I'm looking for Henry Wassman."

I introduced myself and explained that Henry wasn't home. And that he'd probably be away for a while.

"Aha," said Rogga Lundberg. "You're his little brother, aren't you?"

I didn't like him. At first glance, I knew Rogga Lundberg was nothing you'd hang in the Christmas tree and was to be gotten rid of as quickly as possible. Maybe the sunglasses were what gave away his unsavory nature; he didn't bother to remove them even though it was a cloudy day.

And yet, I did admit to being Henry's brother.

"Let's sit down and have a little chat," Rogga Lundberg said. "I know Henry. It'd be fun to get to know his brother, too. Who's your pal?"

"Edmund," Edmund said.

Reluctantly we sat down at the garden table. Rogga lit a cigarette.

"I've worked with Henry a bit," he said. "At *Kurren*. I'm freelance, too."

With that, the word *freelance* lost some of its sheen.

"So, there's a lot going on around here." He gestured toward the woods and the clearing. Edmund and I didn't move a muscle.

"It's not every day there's a murder on our doorstep. Yup, I'm doing some writing about it, you know. One man's death is another man's bread. You read *Kurren*, don't you?"

"We don't know anything about it," I said.

"We just happen to live nearby," said Edmund.

"Really?" said Rogga Lundberg, flashing a smile. "But Henry knows quite a bit, doesn't he?"

"What's that supposed to mean?" I asked.

He didn't answer right away. He clasped his hands behind his neck and leaned back in the chair as if sunning himself. Wearing those damned sunglasses. Even though it was cloudy. He took two drags from his cigarette and then let it hang from the corner of his mouth.

"When's he back, did you say?"

"Late," I said, suddenly reminded of the conversation I'd had with Berra Albertsson less than a week before. It had been almost exactly the same, and this made the hair on the back of my neck bristle with dread. "Won't be back until tonight, probably."

"Does he have nocturnal habits, your brother?"

I didn't respond. Edmund took off his glasses and rubbed the bridge of his nose. A nervous tic.

"Listen," said Rogga Lundberg, sounding serious all of a sudden. "It's just as well you understand what the police are thinking. Or that Henry does. That's why I want to have a word with him."

"Is that so?" I said.

He flicked his cigarette over his shoulder. "Nothing strange about it," he said. "Clever boys like yourselves shouldn't have a problem catching my drift. Especially if you put your heads together."

We didn't respond.

"Berra Albertsson was found up where you park the cars. Right? On the night between Wednesday and Thursday last week?"

I nodded reluctantly.

"Someone beat him to death right as he was getting out of his car. So, the police's first conclusion must be that he'd intended to park there. Can you tell me why?"

"You don't have to answer," Rogga Lundberg continued when neither Edmund nor I showed any sign of speaking. "It's obvious. There's only one reason you'd park up there. Either he was going to visit the Lundins or he was going to visit you ... It's one or the other. There are no other alternatives. What do you have to say about that?"

"Maybe he was stopping for a piss," said Edmund.

"And a madman just happened to be up there," I said.

Rogga Lundberg didn't mind the interruption.

"Let me tell you, that was the police's theory from the start: Super-Berra had planned on coming here—or going to the Lundins' over there ..." He nodded toward the Lundins' place. "And there was someone who wanted to prevent him from getting there. Or here. And they succeeded ... Hmm?"

The question mark after the "hmm" was as clear as day, but neither I nor Edmund made any attempt to reply.

"The police focused on the Lundins first, of course— they're no strangers to this sort of thing. Unfortunately, that was a dead end. In this case, there isn't much pointing to their involvement."

"How c-c-could you know that?" said Edmund. "Y-y-you're talking a lot of shit."

It was the first time I'd heard Edmund stutter. Rogga Lundberg lost track of himself for a second. Then he gave a contemptuous sniff and took out another cigarette.

"This is why I need to talk to Henry, see," he said. "Shame he isn't home. It'll be too bad if we can't have a talk soon."

Cancer-Treblinka-Love-Fuck-Death, I thought for the first time in a long time.

"So you should probably let him know I stopped by and tell him what I said. You can tell him I know about his romantic entanglements, too. One in particular. He'll understand."

He got up and lit a cigarette, looking at us through those dark lenses. Then he shrugged and left.

We stayed put for a long time and tried to forget him. But we couldn't.

It was probably the conversation with Rogga Lundberg that made us tackle the Ewa Kaludis problem that very Wednesday.

Henry was sleeping when we got up. We hadn't heard him come home the previous night, and before we set off we left a note on the kitchen table saying that a colleague had come looking for him. I didn't want to say more; it would be better to tell him the rest when we were back in the evening.

It was a warm but windy day. We left on our bikes in the morning, but Edmund got a flat about halfway between Sjölycke and Åsbro. We had to go down into the village and spend an hour outside of Laxman's with a bucket of water, patches, and rubber solution. Britt Laxman wasn't there; Edmund and I thought it was just as well, and finally we decided the inner tube would be able to hold air again.

The headwind meant that we didn't reach town until around two. We'd called my dad from Laxman's—it was the second of his three weeks of holiday and he hadn't yet gone to the hospital—and said we were thinking of stopping by Idrottsgatan. When we arrived, he'd just started to prepare hamburgers and onions.

His cooking was so-so, as usual, but we were hungry and he looked pleased when we'd eaten up.

"Good, boys. Eat until you burst. You never know where your next meal is coming from."

"Truer words were never spoken," said Edmund.

"Has it settled down out there?" my father wondered.

We nodded. If we let anything slip about Henry and Ewa Kaludis or Rogga Lundberg, he'd lock us in on the spot and forbid us from ever setting foot in Gennesaret again. I felt ashamed about keeping him in the dark and hoped I'd have a chance to explain later.

Somehow. I just didn't know how.

"I'm glad you boys have each other," my father said.

"A burden shared is a burden halved," Edmund said.

We ate rhubarb cream for dessert; my father wondered if I felt like coming along to see my mother, but Edmund and I had a thing or two to take care of. He was fine with that, and we all left Idrottsgatan together. My father, to catch the bus to Örebro. Us, to pay a visit to the fiancée whom the murdered handball star had left behind.

But first we procrastinated for two hours.

We spent the first in the cement pipe and smoked the four loose Ritzes we'd bought at the kiosk at the station when we passed through Hallsberg.

The second we spent sitting on a bench in Brand-station Park fifty meters from the yellow-tiled villa on Hambergsgatan.

It wasn't easy figuring out what we wanted to talk to Ewa Kaludis about. The closer we came to being face-to-face with her, the colder our feet got. We didn't seem to want to admit it to each other, but I noticed Edmund was at least as jittery about seeing her again as I was.

Because Ewa Kaludis might be keeping a lot to herself. She might know things that maybe it was better for two fourteen-year-old admirers not to know.

On the other hand, she might very well need our help, and this was the reason for our gentlemanly relief mission. When all was said and done, there was nothing to suggest that she and my brother Henry had had any contact with each other in the week since the murder—at least, that's what we thought after turning the situation around in our heads, forward, backward, and sideways.

Neither of us wanted to draw a conclusion.

On the other-other hand (and maybe this was what gave us our courage) there was a good chance she wouldn't even be home on a day like this, and we'd be able to go back to Gennesaret with our self-esteem intact and our task unaccomplished.

When the Emmanuel Church's clock struck half-past five, Edmund sighed deeply.

"Screw it," he said. "We're ringing her doorbell. Now."
And so we did.

18

"Erik and Edmund," Ewa Kaludis exclaimed. "So good of you to come. It's been ... no, actually, I don't know."

We could hardly believe we were inside Ewa Kaludis's home. And that she and Super-Berra lived in this gleaming tiled mansion. Well, Super-Berra didn't live here anymore, but his presence was palpable. Framed diplomas hung on the walls and most of the shelves of the large bookcase in the living room were filled with trophies and plaques testifying to what an outstanding athlete he'd been. The coolest one hung above the TV. A huge photograph of Berra Albertsson and Ingemar Johansson. They were both wearing ties and giving the camera crooked and world-weary smiles, so you could tell beyond a shadow of a doubt that these weren't just any old nobodies shaking mitts. I felt a little queasy looking at the picture; it seemed to flicker inside my head.

Otherwise, it was obvious that Ewa was happy about our visit. Like she'd been expecting us. When we'd finished staring at the trophies she led us straight through the house to the back patio where there was a table with a parasol and four chairs. She invited us to sit and asked if we wanted fruit drink and cake.

We did, and she disappeared inside the house again.

"These are quite some digs," said Edmund.

"Mm," I said.

"Did you see Ingo?"

I nodded. Then we sat there, clutching the sun-warmed armrests, which were made of a redolent dark-brown wood, and tried to adapt to our surroundings. It wasn't easy. Of all the friends' houses I'd visited none had been like this, and the tingling in my body and Edmund's grew stronger the longer we sat, waiting, feeling small. I peeked through the balcony door. It was remarkable. Expanses of floor without any furniture. Without a specific function. A glass table. A tree in a huge clay pot. An odd painting with red and blue triangles and circles. Pretty damn remarkable, actually.

And it all looked like it had come straight from the furniture factory last week. I glanced at Edmund; he was having similar thoughts. This place was something else. Berra and Ewa Kaludis were of a different kind, and that got me down—it was as if the insurmountable distance between myself and Ewa had reasserted itself.

Like it ever could have been surmountable.

I'm not sure what I meant by that. My thoughts wandered and spun, and I bit my cheek. How self-involved was I, sitting here thinking these dumb thoughts? Circumstances being what they were.

Ewa returned with a tray that held a jug, glasses, and a small plate with pieces of hedgehog slice.

"So good of you to have come," she repeated and sat across from us. "I've been so worried ... didn't know what ... what to do."

You could still see where his fists had met her face. She was yellowish around the eye with patches of blue and her lower lip was swollen and scabbed.

"Well, we thought ..." said Edmund. "... we'd swing by. Since we were in town anyway."

"And hear how you've been," I added.

Ewa poured the yellow fruit drink for us.

"It's ... I don't understand it," she said.

I wondered what it was she didn't understand, but I didn't say anything.

"We're sorry for your loss," said Edmund.

Ewa looked at him with surprise, like she didn't quite know what he meant.

"Loss?" she said. "Oh, that, of course."

I reached over and took a piece of hedgehog slice. I wondered if she'd made it herself. And if so, had she done it before or after the murder? It tasted pretty fresh, but presumably they had a freezer, so it could be either-or.

"Have you seen Henry lately?" I asked.

She shook her head.

"Not since ... No, not since."

"Oh?" said Edmund. "No, that's probably just as well."

Ewa sighed deeply, and it was only then that I realized just how worried she was. When I dared to look more closely I saw her eyes were quite red, in addition to the yellow and blue, and I guessed that she'd been crying. And recently, too.

"Does he know?" she asked. "Does Henry know you're here?"

"No," Edmund and I said in unison.

"Hm," said Ewa Kaludis, and I couldn't tell if she thought it was good or bad that Henry hadn't sent us.

Maybe she'd been hoping we had a message from him, maybe not. We ate the cake and had our drink.

"It was no good between us," she said. "It was no good between me and Berra. You must be wondering."

"Well," said Edmund.

I said nothing and tied a shoelace that had come undone.

"It couldn't have kept going the way it was, but it didn't have to end like this. I feel so sorry for Henry; it's all my fault. If I'd only known ... even in my wildest imagination, I couldn't have imagined ..."

"What does anyone know," I said.

"Man proposes but God disposes," said Edmund.

"I don't know how I didn't see Bertil for who he was until it was too late," Ewa continued. "How could I not have known it was wrong from the start? When I met your brother, I realized how mad it all was. Dear God, if some things could be undone." She paused and ran her fingers over her swollen lip. "Still, I did love him. If only you could turn back time, just once."

She was talking more to herself now than to Edmund and me. Her words weren't meant for the ears of fourteen-year-old boys, I could tell, and while I was thinking that, I also felt a little sorry for Berra Albertsson.

Well, I didn't feel sorry for him because he was dead. It's just that it couldn't have been much fun to have had the love of a woman like Ewa Kaludis and then wake up one morning to find that love gone.

Even though this flew through my mind for just a split second, I suspected it was one of the few truly deep thoughts I'd had lately.

One of those recurring questions.

If it's better to be loved and then unloved, or not to be subjected to it in the first place.

A "clincher," I think they call it.

"I wander around here not knowing which way is which," said Ewa Kaludis. "I'm sorry I'm going on like this, I'm not really myself."

"We understand," said Edmund. "Sometimes you're stuck in the mud, and don't know how to get out."

Ewa didn't answer. I cleared my throat and took a chance.

"Were you there that night?" I asked.

She took a deep breath and looked at me.

"In Gennesaret?" I clarified.

She looked at Edmund for a while before answering.

"Yes," she said. "I was there."

"Do the police know?" I asked.

She leaned back in the chair and folded her hands in her lap.

"No," she said. "The police don't know anything about Henry and me."

"Good," Edmund said.

"At least I think they don't," Ewa added. "But tell Henry something for me, will you? Give him a message?"

"Of course," I said. "What should we tell him?"

She thought for a moment.

"Tell him," she said. "Tell him that everything will be fine and he shouldn't worry on my behalf."

That didn't seem to jive with how she was really feeling, but I still committed it to memory.

Word for word, her message for Henry, my brother.

Everything will be fine and you shouldn't worry on Ewa Kaludis's behalf.

Before we left, she hugged both of us. Her bare arms and shoulders were hot from the sun and I had the pluck to hug her back properly. I took a long sniff of her skin, and a cloud of Ewa Kaludis unfurled in my head.

It felt fantastic. The swelling cloud floated through me and held the Incident and Cancer-Treblinka and everything else unpleasant at bay for a few hours. Only when we were riding past Laxman's did the cloud disappear. It was immediately replaced by a cold void in my gut.

Like being gripped by an icy fist.

So, maybe, I thought, maybe it would have been better not to inhale Ewa Kaludis's scent.

Maybe it would be easier to sit on the toilet for the rest of my life and forget about putting myself out there. Maybe Edmund's theory about the soul wasn't so crazy after all. It was easy to find, if you could be bothered to pay attention and sense where it was.

Here, on this rough potholed path between Åsbro and Sjölycke, my soul was at the center of my heart.

It seemed to go where it hurt the most. Who knew why.

Henry still hadn't returned by the time we got back to Gennesaret, and that was just as well. I'd have to have a serious talk with him, both about what Rogga Lundberg had said and about our visit to Ewa, but for the moment—in the fatal emptiness beyond that fragrant cloud—I was so crestfallen that I couldn't have even if I'd wanted to.

Edmund wasn't in much better spirits. We ate a few bland hot dogs with bread—no mustard because there wasn't any left—took a quick dip off the dock and went to bed.

"This doesn't feel good, Erik," Edmund said once we'd turned off the light. "How could a summer as brilliant as this one go so wrong? So goddamn wrong."

"Let's sleep on it," I said.

19

"Let's take the boat out," my brother Henry said, and so we did.

Henry rowed and I sat on the thwart. It was another sunny day with a fair amount of wind; we approached the waves at an angle with our course set for Seagull Shit Island. Henry kept missing his strokes and I realized I was actually a much better oarsman than he was. He insisted on smoking while he rowed, which obviously made it much harder for him. When we were about one hundred meters from the island, he lifted the oars out of the water and took off his short-sleeved sweater.

"We need to have a talk," he said.

"Yes," I said. "I suppose we do."

"I didn't know it would turn out this way."

"Me either."

He lit two Lucky Strikes and handed one to me.

"Like I said, no idea."

I nodded.

"What did Rogga Lundberg want?"

I told him about the conversation with Rogga Lundberg, and while I talked Henry ran his hand over his stubble and looked even more blue. When I'd finished he just sat there, staring out at Fläskhällen, where we were slowly drifting.

"Would you say his manner was threatening?" he asked.

I thought about it.

"Yes," I said. "I think it was. I think he wanted to take advantage of you."

"Good," said Henry. "Well done, brother. You can read people. That's not bad for your age; most people never learn. Rogga Lundberg is an asshole. Always has been."

"Like Berra Albertsson?"

Henry laughed.

"Not quite. A different kind. There are many types of asshole, and the trick is knowing what kind you're dealing with."

I nodded. Henry fell silent again. I leaned over the edge of the boat and cupped my hand in a wave. I rinsed my face. Henry watched me and then did the same. It wasn't much, but I felt more equal to him than ever before. I cleared my throat and looked away. I was blushing.

Henry drummed his fingers on his knee. "Anything else?" he asked.

"We visited Ewa yesterday."

For a moment, he looked quite surprised.

"Oh?"

"She sent a message."

He raised an eyebrow.

"We were supposed to tell you that everything will be fine and you don't have to worry on her behalf."

Henry nodded and sank back into his thoughts. Then he cleared his throat and spat in the water.

"That's good," he said. "How nice of you to visit her."

I wondered if I should tell him that she'd seemed worried, but I decided against it. No need to add to his burden. Sufficient unto the day is the evil thereof.

"Well, that settles it," Henry said eventually.

"What do you mean?" I asked.

"Rogga Lundberg," Henry said. "If Rogga knows about Ewa and me, then it's just as well the police find out, too."

"I was gonna suggest that," I said, because I was.

"There's no reason to put your destiny in the hands of someone like him. Remember that, brother. Sometimes you gotta tell the truth. There are no shortcuts, and you have to do it yourself. Do you know where I was yesterday?"

I shook my head. "No."

"With the police." He laughed his short, sharp laugh. "I spent the whole afternoon at the police station in Örebro with Detective Superintendent Lindström and two other detectives. They couldn't agree on whether to let me go or not, but in the end Lindström decided that I could. But I'm barred from traveling."

"A travel ban? How does that work?"

Henry shrugged.

"I can't go anywhere, have to stay close to home ... so it's just as well I talk to them about Ewa."

I thought about it.

"Before they find out from someone else," I said.

"Exactly," said Henry and splashed another handful of water on his face. "Before some asshole or other tries to make a few bucks. I wonder if that bastard's been to see Ewa as well."

"She didn't mention it," I said.

"No," said Henry. "Let's hope he hasn't gotten around to it."

He took hold of the oars again. A few seagulls came flying our way, shrieking. Henry cursed at them; then he gave me a long, serious look before he began to row.

"I don't like talking about this," he said. "And I know

you don't either. But it had to be done. Do we understand each other?"

"I think so," I answered.

Before Henry set off he gave me and Edmund seventy kronor for the shopping. Every last cheese rind in the pantry had been eaten, so we were sorely in need of provisions. On top of that, once Henry was at the police station, he might not return to Gennesaret—if they'd been unsure of him yesterday, then he'd hardly be better off after admitting to having relations with the deceased's fiancée.

It was just like a Perry Mason story, Edmund and I concurred, after I told him about the conversation.

Except that Perry himself was nowhere to be found.

We took the bikes out that day, spent every last coin at Laxman's, and on the way back Edmund told me more about his real dad.

About how he used to cry.

"Cry?" I said. "What do you mean, cry?"

"When he was hitting me," said Edmund. "Or after. When he was done. Sometimes he did, anyway."

"Why'd he cry?"

"I don't know," Edmund said. "I've never understood it. He would sit on his bed sniffling and saying it hurt him more than it hurt me, and that I'd understand when I got older."

"What were you supposed to understand?"

Edmund shrugged so sharply he lost his balance and almost fell over his handlebars. He regained control of the bike and swore. "How the hell should I know? Why he had to beat me up, I suppose. As if there was a reason, but I was too young to understand ... that he was hitting me against his will somehow. As if something were forcing him to and he couldn't be held responsible ..."

We pedaled in silence.

"That's weird," I said. "Hitting someone on purpose, then crying about it."

"He was sick," said Edmund. "What else can I say? Sick from the worms crawling around and eating up his brain or something like that."

"Sounds like a load of baloney," I said, but deep inside—deep down in an underdeveloped part of my fourteen-year-old brain—I suspected that those people did in fact exist.

People who cried over what they did and for those to whom they did it.

I didn't like it. This idea contradicted what Henry and I had talked about.

Sometimes you gotta tell the truth.

No, I had no desire to think about stuff like Edmund's dad. As I said, I'd made that choice long ago. Cancer-Treblinka-Love-Fuck-Death.

No further questions.

20

My brother Henry was charged with the murder of Bertil "Berra" Albertsson on Thursday July nineteenth, and it was in the papers on Friday.

It was also on that Friday that Detective Superintendent Verner Lindström paid me and Edmund another visit. By nine in the morning, he'd arrived with a few copies of the *Läns* newspaper, where he had us read about the developments in the case, before interrogating us.

Henry's name wasn't given, he was either called "the accused" or "the suspect" and there was no mention of him having gone to the police of his own volition.

And neither was there anything about what had made him a suspect in the first place. All it said was that the suspect had "certain relations" with the victim. The charge was the result of laborious and fruitful investigative work, but the young man hadn't confessed to anything, Detective Lindström had said during a short press conference on Thursday evening.

There wasn't much more to it.

"False information has been given about this case," Lindström said when we'd finished reading. "By you two, for instance. This time I want the truth, gentlemen. The whole truth."

He sounded much rougher than before. Like sandpaper or something. Edmund folded the newspaper and pushed it back across the table.

"And nothing but the truth," Edmund said in English.

"You can go wait outside for now," Lindström said. "Stay close. And stick to Swedish from here on in."

Edmund's cheeks went a little red, and he left us alone in the kitchen.

Lindström took out the tube of Bronzol but didn't open it. He just set it on the table and rolled it back and forth with his right index and middle fingers. Apparently, he didn't need a notebook this time around; I didn't really know how I was supposed to interpret that.

I didn't know how I was supposed to interpret the silence either, the one he filled with the sound of his breath flowing through his hairy nostrils while watching me, no more than an arm's length away. He was like a cold sun lamp; I looked between the Bronzol and my hands, which I was wringing in my lap.

"You and your brother," he finally began.

"Yes?" I said.

"What's it like between the two of you?"

"Good," I said.

"He's quite a bit older than you."

That didn't sound like a question, so I didn't respond.

"How much older?"

"Just over eight years."

"Would you say that you know him well?"

"Sure," I said.

"You know about the kinds of things he gets up to?"

"Oh yes."

"What does he do?"

"Journalism," I said. "He's freelance. But he's taken time off this summer to write a book."

"A book?"

"Yes."

"What kind of book?"

"A novel," I said. "About life."

"Life?"

"Yes."

Lindström tapped the tube on the table, but still he didn't open it.

"How does he do with the ladies?"

I shrugged and looked uninterested. "Good, I suppose."

"Who's Emmy Kaskel?"

"Emmy? His ex-fiancée."

"Ex?"

"Yes."

"And who's his fiancée now?"

I looked at his blue polka-dot bow tie. Had it been a Christmas present from his wife? Did he even have a wife?

"No one, I think."

"Really?"

I didn't answer.

"How does Ewa Kaludis fit in, then?"

"She was our substitute teacher this spring," I said.

"I know she was your substitute teacher," said Lindström. "You said so last time. Now I want to know what kind of relationship she had with your brother Henry."

"I think they knew each other," I said.

"Aha," said Lindström. "So you think they knew each other. How come you didn't say so last time?"

"You didn't ask," I said.

He paused and his breathing was the only sound. He studied the fingers on his left hand, as though checking for dirt under the nails.

"How old did you say you were?"

"I didn't."

"So tell me."

"Fourteen."

"Fourteen? Only fourteen years old, and you think you need to protect your twenty-two-year-old brother?"

"I'm not trying to protect my brother. I don't know what you mean."

Lindström's mouth twitched.

"You know very well what I mean," he said. "You've always known that Henry was involved with Ewa Kaludis, and you think you're helping him by keeping that to yourself."

"That's not so," I said.

Lindström ignored my interjection. He was on a roll, and it was feeling like a real cross-examination.

"You think you're helping Henry by keeping quiet about what you know," he explained. "You're not. You're on the wrong track, just like your friend. Henry told us everything and having his little brother try to blindside us will only hurt him."

"I told you they knew each other."

He opened the tube and tossed back two pastilles.

"How many times has she been here?"

I shrugged. "A couple. Three maybe."

"At what time?"

"I don't remember. Evenings, I think."

"Nights?"

"Maybe."

"This July?"

I thought about it. "Yeah, maybe."

He leaned back and looked out the window. He seemed tired all of a sudden. He probably hadn't been sleeping much lately. He probably had a lot on his plate. He chewed the pastilles, then continued speaking.

"So Ewa Kaludis spent a couple or more nights here in the house with your brother Henry at the beginning of July. Are we in agreement on that point?"

I gave a slight nod.

"You knew that Ewa Kaludis was Bertil Albertsson's fiancée?"

"Yes."

"Didn't you think it was strange that she was sleeping here with your brother instead of with her fiancé?"

"I didn't think about it much."

He studied the nails on his other hand.

"The ninth of July," he then said. "Tell me about the ninth of July."

"What day was that?" I asked.

"Wednesday last week. The day before the night Bertil Albertsson was murdered."

I thought for a good while.

"I don't really remember," I said. "It wasn't anything special, I think."

"You remembered it well the last time we spoke."

"I did?"

His fist hitting the table was like a gunshot. I flinched and almost fell backwards in my chair. I caught myself on the table top at the last second and found my balance again.

"Enough messing around," Lindström snapped, his voice coarser than sandpaper now. "We know Henry had Ewa Kaludis over that night, and we know that you know. If you want to make things even the slightest bit easier for your brother, you need to tell us what happened. Everything you're holding back. The way you're going, you're making it worse for him."

I didn't reply right away. I counted backward from ten

to zero and avoided looking at him.

"You're wrong," I said. "I have no idea if Ewa Kaludis was here that night. We fell asleep early, both Edmund and I, and I didn't wake once during the night."

Detective Lindström put the Bronzol tube in his jacket's inner pocket. Buttoned all three jacket buttons and put his elbows on the table. I met his gaze. Five seconds passed. I aged a decade.

"Go and get your friend," said Lindström.

After I had taken two steps out onto the lawn, he changed his mind.

"Stop!" he called. "I'll get him myself."

"Of course, detective," I said, changing course and heading for the lake.

Edmund looked downhearted when he laid down beside me on the dock half an hour later.

"Is he gone?" I asked.

Edmund nodded.

"Unbelievable," he said. "They're thinking of locking him up for it."

"He'll be fine," I said.

"You think?" said Edmund.

"Henry always comes out on top."

"I hope you're right," said Edmund.

We lay there. It had been cloudy in the morning, but now the sun was breaking through and it was getting hotter. The dock was swaying slowly and clucking in the waves.

I was a little curious about what Detective Lindström had asked Edmund, and about what Edmund had said, but I didn't want to discuss it.

So I asked: "Should we take a trip to Seagull Shit Island … while we still can?"

Edmund sat up and dipped his feet in the water.

"Sure," he said. "Let's do it. They'll be picking us up soon, don't you think?"

"Probably," I said. "It won't be long."

Edmund sighed and squinted at the lake.

"One last boat trip," he said. "It's too sad for words. It really was one hell of a good summer."

"It was," I said. "Yes, it was."

Our fathers were already waiting for us by the time we'd begun rowing back to shore. They'd been there for over an hour and our things were out on the lawn, packed and ready to go.

"You're coming with us to town," said my father. "It's enough now."

Albin Wester said nothing, and it looked as though he had sold all the prisoners at the Gray Giant and then lost the money. Edmund and I changed our clothes and ten minutes later we left Gennesaret. This time my dad had borrowed an old Citroën from the Bergmans, who lived two doors down on Idrottsgatan. It was an old jalopy and, even though we only had to drive twenty-five kilometers, we had to stop twice because the water in the radiator started boiling.

"We could have taken our bikes," said Edmund.

"We'll get the bikes later," Edmund's dad said, irritated. "You know there are more important things to think about right now, don't you?"

"French cars aren't built for the Swedish summer heat," my father said. Then he burned himself on the radiator cap.

21

The weeks after Henry was taken into custody had a strange quality to them. Although the world was upside down and it felt like all sorts of things were happening, it was still pretty monotonous.

Almost every day my father and I drove Killer into Örebro. First we visited Henry at the police station, then my mother at the hospital. The very fact that my father, not Henry, was driving Killer was a sure sign that things were out of whack. My father probably didn't really fit in anywhere, but he stuck out like a sore thumb behind the wheel of the black vw. Under normal circumstances he was a terrible driver, in Killer his driving was catastrophic; I remember thinking more than once: "Here we go again," and, "The last thing we need now is a car accident. On top of everything else."

Still, we got through each day with our hides intact. Off to Örebro in the morning and back again in the evening. None of us had much to say during those visits to Henry's pale yellow cell in the police station's basement, not me, not my father or my brother. There was a bed attached to the wall, a small table, two chairs, and a lamp. Henry was usually lying on the bed, my father and I sat on the chairs. Every day my father brought a copy of

Kurren with him and a pack of Lucky Strikes and every day Henry's sock had a hole by his right big toe. I started to wonder if he ever changed his socks, but I didn't want to ask.

"How are they allowed to treat honest people this way? They should be ashamed of themselves," my father would say.

Or: "This time tomorrow, you'll be out of here, you'll see."

Henry rarely commented. Usually he'd start reading *Kurren* as soon as we'd sat down, smoking ardently, as if he'd gone without cigarettes for days.

After our visit to the slammer, we'd go to the bakery. Three Roses or New Pomona on Rudbecksgatan. My father would drink coffee with his cinnamon bun, I'd have a Pommac and a rosette, or a Pommac and a Mazarin tart.

"I've taken some extra vacation days," my father would explain halfway through his cinnamon bun each day. "I thought I might as well, until this sorts itself out."

"It's been a rough summer," I'd reply.

At the hospital everything was the same except for two things: my mother looked much worse, and my father had started crying at her bedside.

When I saw it coming, I'd usually make a point of going to the toilet. It was a pretty nice one—large and spacious. The walls were adorned with small not-quite-square tiles and while I sat there with my trousers and pants pushed down around my ankles, I tried to play tic tac toe against myself in my head. It was very hard, considering the tiles weren't quite square, and I was never really on board with beating myself at my own game.

"You're being a good boy, Erik?" my mother would ask before we left her.

"Yes, I am," I'd promise.

"Keep your courage up," she'd say. "Once you let it drop, it'll be too heavy to pick back up."

And then my father and I would nod earnestly.

Truer words were never spoken.

I think it was Wednesday when a piece about the Berra Albertsson murder first appeared in *Kurren*. It was signed "R.L."

Rogga Lundberg didn't mention Henry by name, but he wrote about Gennesaret and about Ewa Kaludis, and wrote that the perpetrator who was now in police custody in Örebro was most likely a former reporter for the newspaper. The article also said that the motive behind the gruesome deed had been established and it was a so-called "crime of passion."

And that it was only a matter of time before Detective Lindström and his capable men would crack the accused and extract a confession.

A confession of his infamous deed.

Henry kept bursting into laughter as he read Rogga Lundberg's article. He was laughing so hard my father and I wondered if everything was all right with him.

Could he be crumbling under the pressure? Was he about to crack, just as Rogga Lundberg had predicted?

"Pressure?" Henry asked when my worried father asked him how he was doing. "As if I'd take what that arch-cretin writes seriously. What do you take me for? I thought we were related?"

I didn't know what an "arch-cretin" was, but it was something of a relief to hear Henry respond like that.

My father seemed to think so, too, because that day he didn't cry at the hospital, and in the car on the way home he said:

"That's some kid, Erik. You can't keep him down."

Soon after he said that, he overtook a car for the first time in five days.

Edmund and I met only one other time that summer: when Lasse Side-Smile's dad had driven his Ford van to the town square to deliver our bikes the Sunday after we left Gennesaret. I asked Edmund if he wanted to come to Idrottsgatan for a bit, but he said he had to hurry home and pack. His dad had arranged for him to spend the rest of the summer vacation at his cousins' in Mora.

Edmund had told me about his cousins once when we rowed to Laxman's, and he'd described them as two deaf-mute bed-wetters with underbites. Now they seemed to have grown into themselves a bit; Edmund thought he'd probably have an all right time up there.

"They have rabbits and everything."

"Rabbits?" I said.

"And everything," said Edmund, fidgeting.

We said "See you later" and wished each other luck.

About a week after Henry was taken into custody, my dad and I went back to Gennesaret to pick up whatever had been left behind. Clothes and groceries and so on. It was raining buckets the entire time we were there and we stayed no longer than necessary. When my father looked through the shed, he noticed the sledgehammer was missing. He called me over to ask if we'd used it.

"Not that I remember," I said. "Maybe when we were building the dock?"

"Take a look around and see if you can find it," my father said.

I went out in the rain and looked for it, then explained that I couldn't find it and I didn't know where it could have got to. My father had a strange look in his eyes, but didn't say anything. He just stood there, staring at me as if he'd never seen anything like me before.

As if I were a rebus—yes, that's what came to mind standing there in the kitchen at Gennesaret that rainy day. I was a rebus my dad had been trying to solve my whole life and now he was getting close. Maybe all people were rebuses to each other, and some of us were rebuses to ourselves.

It didn't take much time. We locked up, and jogged up the path to the parking spot with our luggage and our grocery bags. Loaded them into Killer and drove off. About halfway to Hallsberg, my father asked:

"You don't have to answer. You absolutely do not have to answer, but do you think he did it?"

I considered his question and said:

"How could you think your own son is a murderer?"

Henry's typewriter and his stack of typed pages were among the things we brought home from Gennesaret. That evening I counted the sheets of paper in the pile: there were eighty-five pages. There were quite a few strike-throughs and additions made in ballpoint pen. If this is what my older brother's handwriting looked like, perhaps it was no wonder that mine—a source of constant frustration for Brylle and the others at Stava School—looked like chicken scratch, too.

I wondered about the page that had been left in the typewriter, the one I'd read and committed to memory a few weeks earlier. The one about the body and the gravel road and the summer night. I leafed through the stack of paper three times without finding it. I tried to remember it word for word, but so much had happened since that I'd lost it.

I only remembered that it had been beautiful. Beautiful, surprising, and a little frightening.

The next day we brought both the Facit and the typescript to Henry, because he'd asked for them. And a new packet of typing paper. You could tell he was eager for us to leave so he could start writing.

I thought it was a good sign that he wanted to sit down and start clattering away again.

In spite of it all, there was hope.

One evening a few days later I ran into Ewa Kaludis. I'd gone to Törner's for a hot-dog special because my father didn't have it in him to cook, and I could have sworn she was there waiting for me. It was right by Nilsson's Cycle and Sport on the corner of Mossbanegatan and Östra Drottninggatan, and as far as I knew she had no other reason to be right there. No apparent reason, anyway.

"Hi, Erik," she said.

"Hi," I said, and stopped.

She was wearing the Swanson shirt and those black slacks again. And the hairband. Her bruises were barely visible and I was struck once again by how terribly beautiful she was.

So beautiful it hurt, I'd almost managed to forget about it.

"Where are you going?" she asked.

"Home," I said.

"Are you in a rush or can we have a word? We can walk in your direction."

"Sure," I said. "I'm in no rush."

We started to walk along Mossbanegatan. Even though I was only fourteen years old I was as tall as she was, and I got it into my head that from a distance people might think we were a couple out for a stroll. A young man and his woman. My head was spinning with this thought and because she was so close to me.

And because we'd walked quite a ways before she said anything. Almost all the way to Snukke's old asbestos-ridden house.

"I'm afraid," she said.

"Of what?" I asked.

"Of visiting Henry at the police station."

"Why? It's not bad; I go every day."

"It's not that. I'm thinking about what the police would make of it."

"I see," I said. "Well, I don't know what they're thinking."

"Neither do I," said Ewa. "And I don't want them to get the wrong idea."

I wondered what idea they might get that they didn't already have. I didn't know what could possibly make this situation any worse.

But I didn't ask what she meant.

"Would you give him this letter for me?" she asked as we neared Karlesson's shop.

I took the sealed envelope, which had neither name nor address written on it. All that distinguished it was that it was light blue.

We didn't say much else, but before we parted I plucked up the courage. An incredible courage. I don't know where it came from.

I stood before Ewa Kaludis. Our faces were no more than twenty centimeters apart. I reached out both of my hands and placed them on her upper arms.

"Ewa," I said. "I don't care that I'm only fourteen years old. You're the most beautiful woman on earth and I love you."

She gasped.

"I had to say it," I said. "That's all. Thank you very much."

Then I kissed her and walked away.

I dreamed of Ewa Kaludis for the rest of the summer. Images of her making love to my brother Henry came to me and sometimes I was the one who was lying there instead of Henry. Often I was in two places at once: both outside the window and underneath Ewa. Underneath her and inside her. When I woke in the mornings I couldn't always remember whether or not I'd dreamed of her, but all I had to do was check if there were fresh stains on the sheets to find out. More often than not there were.

Of course it wasn't easy keeping her out of my thoughts during the days either; I made a point of fantasizing about her while I was in the toilet at the hospital. It was a good alternative to tic tac toe, and sometimes I'd think about her when we were in Killer on our way to Örebro.

I'm going to the slammer to see my brother Henry. Then I'm going to visit my dying mother in the hospital and to think about Ewa Kaludis and jerk myself off.

When I thought about it like that, I felt ashamed.

Orientation at Kumla County Junior Secondary School was on August twenty-seventh and it was the same day my brother was remanded in custody. I was in a class called I:3 B with thirty-two new classmates and had a homeroom teacher with a lisp called Gunvald, who was one of my thirteen new teachers. I was subjected to a string of hitherto unknown subjects like physics, chemistry, German, and morning assembly, and generally gained new perspectives on life.

One Friday, about a month into the school year, Henry turned up. He was waiting for me outside the school gates when we'd finished for the day. I walked out with a handful of classmates I didn't know very well, and they fell silent around me. Of course everyone knew who Henry was, and his sudden appearance reminded them that I was the murderer's brother.

I went up to him. He was wearing sunglasses, an unbuttoned nylon shirt, and had a Lucky Strike hanging from the corner of his mouth. He was the spitting image of Ricky Nelson. Or Rick.

"Hi, Henry," I said.

"Hi, brother," Henry said, smiling his crooked smile. "How's it going?"

"I'm having a helluva time," I said. "Did they let you out?"

"Yep," said Henry. "It's over now."

He put his arm around my shoulder. We walked across the street and climbed into Killer. My new friends stayed by the school gate, standing around like they'd just dropped out of the sky and didn't know what to do with themselves.

Henry fired up Killer and we drove away leaving a cloud of dust in our wake. I thought about what he'd said at the start of June.

Life should be like a butterfly on a summer's day.

Autumn was a bridge leading to new territory. I never quite got a foothold at KJCSS. Edmund also went there, but he was in another class and we didn't socialize. I didn't really socialize with anyone anymore. Not with people I knew already and not with new people. Sure Benny and I hung out in the cement pipe and chatted some, but it wasn't like before. We grew apart and it happened more quickly than I could comprehend.

Generally, I did all my homework and was quite the model student, I think. I got an A-plus on my first German exam and an AB on my math test. I finished *Colonel*

Darkin and the Mysterious Heiress, but didn't start on another adventure. I read books, mostly English and American detective stories, and started listening to Radio Luxembourg. I dreamed about Ewa Kaludis but never saw her.

Every so often *Kurren* would run an article about the murder of Berra Albertsson and the police's efforts to find the perpetrator. One Saturday they ran a lengthy summary of the case with maps and Xs where the body had been found and all that, but no new clues or suspects were reported. The police kept working on the case and Detective Lindström spoke to the newspaper in optimistic terms, claiming it was only a matter of time until the murderer would be behind bars.

I don't know if *Kurren*'s regular readers believed him. I certainly had my doubts.

Henry moved to Gothenburg in early November, and on December third my mother died. My father had been at her side during her last ten days, but I couldn't cope.

The funeral was a week later in Kumla's church. I had never worn a suit before. About twenty of us followed my mother to her final resting place: Henry, my father, and I sat on the first pew in the church; behind us sat relatives, a few colleagues, Benny's mother and father, and Mr. Wester.

I'd cried the whole night long, and by the time I got to the church, I didn't have any tears left in me.

III

22

The following February, my father applied for a job at AB Slotts, and at Easter we moved to Uppsala. I was fourteen going on fifteen when I left my childhood home and arrived in the city of mustard and learning. I went to Cathedral School along with the children of senior lecturers and doctors, let my hair grow, and acquired pimples and a record player.

The first year, we lived in a cramped one-bedroom apartment behind Östra Station, and then we moved to Glimmervägen in Eriksberg, a newly built residential area. We had a two-bedroom apartment with a view from the balcony of rocky slopes and a forest. My father perked up a bit; his shifts at the mustard factory were difficult, but the atmosphere was more relaxed there than at the prison. He made a number of new friends at work, started playing bridge once a week, and cautiously pursued a friendship with a widow in Salabacke. As for me, I soon fell in love with a dark-haired girl who lived in the building next to ours, and the summer I turned sixteen I lost my virginity on a blanket in Hågadalen while listening to "The House of the Rising Sun" on the transistor radio she'd brought along. I'm not sure if she was losing hers then too, but she said she was.

Henry kept living in Gothenburg and was given increasingly secure employment at the *Göteborgs Posten* newspaper. Two years and two months after Berra Albertsson's murder, his debut novel *Coagulated Love* was published by Norstedts. It was well received by both the *Svenska Dagbladet* and *Dagens Nyheter*, and his own newspaper gave it a decent review, but Henry never wrote another book. I read *Coagulated Love* over the Christmas vacation that same year and again a few years later, but I didn't get much out of it on either read. When my father died in 1976 I found his signed copy of the book among his possessions; although all of the pages had been sliced open, there was a grocery receipt being used as a bookmark between pages eighteen and nineteen.

My aunt, the victim of the moose-based tragedy, died in the Dingle asylum a few weeks before I graduated from high school; we managed to sell Gennesaret at a pretty decent price, and when I started studying philosophy in the fall, I was able to move into my own one-and-a-half-room flat on Geijersgatan. By this time, my virginity was but a distant memory. Even though I didn't look as much like Rick Nelson as my brother, I still had good luck with the opposite sex; female students came and went and then there was one who stayed.

She was called Ellinor and by the early eighties we'd managed to bring three children into the world. At that point Geijersgatan was also but a memory. We'd bought a house in Norby among the bourgeoisie and the boxwood; I taught history and philosophy at a high school, and when Ellinor wasn't at home raising our children, she was employed as a lab assistant at a pharmaceutical company out in Boländerna.

One May evening in the mid-eighties *Expressen* ran a

two-page article about unsolved murders in Sweden, with a focus on cases where the statute of limitations was running out in a year or so.

One of these was Bertil Albertsson's murder. We were sitting out in the garden, Ellinor and I, the lilacs were about to bloom, and for the first time I told her what had happened at Gennesaret. Once I got going, I realized just how much it fascinated my wife, and I tried to draw as much as I could out of my memory's well. Leaving out the odd detail, of course—even though we had an open and uninhibited relationship, I still felt embarrassed about how Edmund and I had masturbated by the window as Henry and Ewa Kaludis were making love inside. For instance.

When I finished talking, my wife asked:

"And Edmund? How did it go for Edmund?"

I shrugged.

"I don't have the faintest idea, actually."

My wife gave me a bewildered look and wrinkled her forehead, most likely signaling that she'd once again been exposed to some sort of deep-seated male mystery.

"My God," she said. "You mean you lost touch, just like that?"

"My mother died," I pointed out. "We moved."

My wife grabbed the newspaper and re-read the summary of the murder. Then she leaned back in the deck chair and gave the matter some thought.

"We'll look him up," she said. "We'll look him up and invite him to dinner."

"Like hell we will," I said.

To my surprise, getting a hold of Edmund Wester was no problem. Personally, I didn't lift a finger in the search, but in early June, just before graduation, Ellinor told me that she'd found him and he was going to come over and eat crayfish with us in August.

"You went behind my back," I said. "Admit it."

"Of course, dear eagle," my wife answered. "Sometimes foolish men need to be circumvented."

"Where's he living?" I asked. "How'd you reach him?"

"It wasn't hard," my wife explained. "He's a priest in Ånge."

I couldn't help but smile. Norrland again.

"He sounded friendly and genuinely happy to hear from me. He thought it was about time you met up again. You should have plenty to talk about, he said."

"Really?" I said. "Well, don't get your hopes up."

"He's coming out this way in August anyhow," said my wife. "It'll be interesting meeting him, in any case. You know, I've never met anyone from your childhood."

"You've met my father," I pointed out. "And Henry."

My wife waggled her finger.

"They don't count," she said. "Your father is dead. And I've seen your brother a whole three times."

She had a point. My father had been dead for almost a decade by then, and I hadn't been in contact with Henry at all since he emigrated to Uruguay at the end of the seventies. His most recent Christmas card had arrived four years ago on Maundy Thursday.

That year during the first week of the summer vacation I spent most of my time reflecting on my childhood, and one hot, fragrant night I dreamed of Ewa Kaludis for the first time in twenty years. Oddly, it wasn't an erotic dream; it was filled with images and impressions from the day after she'd been beaten up and had sat in the deck chair massaging my shoulders.

Anyway, I thought it was strange when I woke up. And a bit of a shame, but you don't get to choose your dreams, now do you?

Only a few weeks before Edmund's visit did I realize that if he'd joined the priesthood he must have studied in Uppsala. I stayed in that university town for a long time, so we would have been near each other as adults, Edmund and I. At least for a few years. I mulled this over. Had we ever crossed paths in town—when I was a student, perhaps?—and why wouldn't we have recognized each other? I brought this up with my wife, but she said a person can change quite a bit between the ages of fourteen and twenty and it was the rule rather than the exception that you missed people in a crowd.

When Edmund Wester turned up I saw that she was dead right.

When I opened the door the gargantuan, heavily bearded man standing on our steps reminded me as much of fourteen-year-old Edmund as a duck reminds me of a sparrow. I did some rough math in my head and concluded that if his weight gain had followed a steady trajectory then he'd have put on about five kilos a year since I'd last seen him at school in Kumla. It wasn't just the beard hiding the clerical collar, but his double chins. His ragged corduroy suit had room for another three to four years of growth at the same rate.

"Erik Wassman, I presume?" he said, hiding the bouquet for my wife behind his back.

"Edmund," I said. "You haven't changed one bit."

The evening was more pleasant than I'd dared hope. In each of our professions, we'd learned to make both frivolous and serious small talk, and the crayfish were truly exquisite—my wife had made her signature marinade. Our children behaved quite well and went to bed without kicking up too much of a fuss. We drank beer and wine and schnapps and cognac, and any disappointment Ellinor might have felt about our reluctance to discuss the summer in Gennesaret eventually ebbed away.

It's not that we didn't mention Berra Albertsson and the murder, but both Edmund and I were eager to change the subject whenever she brought it up. I remember how we'd kept the same distance when it was all going on, and realized how easy it was to pick up where you had left off with some people, even after such a long time.

If my wife hadn't brought up the subject of a priest's vow of silence and crises of conscience, it would have been a wholly successful night. Unfortunately, we were already in deep when I noticed that Edmund was troubled by the question.

We were well into the coffee and cognac too, so perhaps my lapse in concentration was to be expected.

"It's never made sense to me," my wife said. "What gives a priest the right to keep quiet about things us regular people have to spill? Things we would be punished for?"

"It's not that simple," said Edmund.

"It couldn't be any simpler," my wife said. "What kind of God keeps murderers and miscreants under his wing?"

"There is more than one law," said Edmund. "And more than one judge."

"Isn't our legal system built on Christian ethics?" she insisted. "Isn't the West built on a Christian system of values? Isn't that clause a construct that's ready for the scrap heap?"

Edmund sat quietly and scratched his beard, suddenly grave. I introduced a fresh topic, but wasn't quick enough.

"There are cases," he said. "There will always be situations where a person needs to unburden their heart ... We could never impose a vow of silence on everyone. However, we need some people to have taken one. There have to be options. Someone who listens; someone to whom you can turn and bend the ear of when the need is most pressing. With whom your words are received and sealed-off."

"I don't understand it," said my wife.

"It's a difficult question," Edmund repeated. "There have been moments when I've had my doubts."

He left shortly thereafter. We promised to keep in touch, but it was clear to all three of us that the sentiment was mostly a concession to custom.

After he left, my wife and I sat in our armchairs for a while.

"It has something to do with the Gennesaret murder," she burst out. She poured a finger of cognac for each of us.

"I've had enough cognac, thanks. But what do you mean?"

"The crisis of conscience, of course. His discomfort with the question. It's related to the murder of Bertil Albertsson twenty years ago."

"Twenty-three," I said. "Oh, nonsense."

"It has nothing to do with being part of the clergy."

"How much have you had to drink?" I asked. "Of course something's happened to him. Someone's confessed to a crime and he doesn't feel he can go to the police. Every priest is bound to face that conflict at some point. It wasn't particularly polite of you to bring it up."

My wife sipped her cognac, thinking.

"All right," she said. "It was rude of me, but I don't think I'm wrong. He's very nice, whatever the case."

"I liked him then, too," I said.

For about a week I was preoccupied by what had been said and what was left unsaid between Edmund, my wife, and me. I finally called him in Ånge and got straight to the point.

"You know what happened that night, don't you?"

"Whatever do you mean?" Edmund asked indignantly.

"I mean, when you went out for a pee, for instance. That wasn't all, was it?"

There was a pause. The phone line crackled and, for a moment, I believed it was the sound of Edmund's thought processes materializing rather than the poor connection.

"I have no reason to discuss this with you any further," he finally said. "But I'd like to ask you the same question, if you don't mind. Do you know who killed Berra Albertsson?"

"How would I know?" I answered crossly. "I was asleep, you know that perfectly well."

There we were, on the phone, not saying anything. Then we hung up.

Perhaps one could describe running into Ewa Kaludis that very autumn as an event that looked like a fantasy.

During a conference about educational materials, I stayed at a hotel in Gothenburg for two nights and, whereas I'd had a hard time recognizing Edmund after several decades, I had no problem recognizing Ewa. No problem at all.

She was standing behind the reception desk when I checked in, and time didn't seem to have left a mark. She had the same beautiful posture. Same high cheekbones. Same crescent eyes. Her blond hair was now red, a hue that suited her even better—I imagined it was her natural color. Though she was surely approaching fifty, she was still an astonishing beauty.

At least in my opinion.

"Dear God." The words slipped from me. "Ewa Kaludis."
She looked at the list of reservations.

"Aha, you've arrived," she said. "Yes, I saw your name."

Ever since we'd exchanged our marriage vows, Ellinor and I had been unswervingly faithful, but I knew I was about to break them. I knew this was about to happen not just because I wanted to, but because—more importantly—I could tell Ewa wanted it, too. She called in to the reception area and ordered a young blond girl to take her place at the desk; she clearly held some sort of managerial position at the hotel. Then she flipped up the counter and walked over to me.

"I'll show you to your room," she said. "What fun to see you again after all these years."

We rode the elevator up.

"Do you remember the last thing you said to me that summer?" she asked when we were in the room.

I nodded.

"And what you did?"

I nodded again.

"Do you still have that fourteen-year-old inside of you?"

"Every single inch of him," I answered.

She'd just had her period—and was a bit preoccupied—so on the first night we just talked.

"I want to thank you for what you did that summer," said Ewa. "Thank you and Edmund for how you acted afterward and so on. There was never really the right moment to say it."

"I loved you," I explained. "I think Edmund loved you, too."

She smiled.

"It was Henry who loved me. And I loved Henry."

I asked how it had gone between her and my brother. If anything had happened in the end, or if it had all run out with the sand after the Incident.

"We did meet up eventually," she said after a pause. "Here in Gothenburg. More than a year later. We didn't dare before. Then we were together for a while. Did he never tell you?"

I shook my head.

"I've barely had any contact with my brother. He moved and we moved."

"It never really worked," she continued. "I don't know why, but what happened, well, it—the Incident, as you call it—was in the way."

I nodded. I understood. I could see how it would've been strange if it had worked out. I hadn't thought about it that way when I was fourteen, sitting across from Detective Lindström, but now it seemed logical that not only had nothing lasting transpired between Henry and Ewa, but also there was a reason for it.

A kind of justice.

"Are you married?" I asked.

She shook her head.

"Was. I have a fourteen-year-old daughter. That's why I don't have much time tonight."

"I remember your hands on my shoulders," I said. "And I want to make love to you tomorrow night. To try at least."

She laughed.

"I have time tomorrow," she agreed. "I'll try to meet your expectations, otherwise I think it will be enough to be able to sleep together."

Sleeping wasn't enough. The night between the sixteenth and seventeenth of October I made love to Ewa

Kaludis after waiting for over twenty years.

Making love to her for the first time was the most serious undertaking of my life, and I think the feeling was mutual. In the following year we met up a number of times—at ever more frequent intervals—and one month after the divorce with Ellinor came through, I moved to Gothenburg. I managed to secure a decent job at a high school out in Mölndal and by early 1987 we were finally living under the same roof.

Me, Ewa Kaludis, and her daughter Karla.

"It feels like coming home," I told Ewa that first night.

"Welcome home," said Ewa.

Not many weeks passed before I had to tell her how Edmund and I had watched as she'd made love with Henry that night. I'd only been an immature fourteen-year-old at the time, so I hoped she'd understand.

When I'd finished the story she put her hand over her mouth and wouldn't look at me. At first I was worried, but then I noticed she was laughing.

"What's going on with you?" I asked.

She grew serious, lowered her hand, and took a deep breath.

"I saw you," she said. "I didn't want to say, but I knew all along that you were standing there."

"Oh dear God," I moaned. "No. Impossible."

"Anything is possible," said Ewa Kaludis and started laughing again.

23

Verner Lindström hadn't gotten any younger.

"The statute of limitations will run out on the case in two months," he explained as he adjusted his bow tie. "But that's not why I want to talk to you. I'm working on a little memoir. I retired in the spring and a person has to keep busy somehow."

We sat in the innermost room at Linnaeus, a restaurant on Linnégatan. As far as I knew Lindström had taken the train down to Gothenburg just for this conversation; he was clearly having a hard time getting through his days in retirement.

It is what it is, I thought. Some people never learn to enjoy their leisure time; others seem made for it.

After we'd eaten Lindström took out his Bronzol tube. I couldn't remember seeing those pastilles in the last ten or fifteen years, but maybe he'd bought a lifetime supply in the early seventies.

"The fact of the matter is," he said and put two pastilles in his mouth. "The fact of the matter is that I don't have many unsolved cases to investigate. Just one murder. Bertil Albertsson."

"Such is life," I said. "Well, you did your best."

He chewed and rocked his head slowly from side to

side like an old, weary bloodhound. "The outcome," he said. "I don't give a damn about all the effort; it's the outcome that counts. Someone murdered that damn handball player on that damn clearing twenty-five years ago and in two months he'll get off scot-free."

"Someone?" I said. "I thought you'd decided it was my brother. You just weren't able to lock him up."

Verner Lindström sighed.

"He or she," he said. "That was the thread we were following. Let me tell you, we spared no expense looking into her either. We spent a good part of that fall interrogating her night and day, but she didn't crack. Damn fine woman. I wonder what happened to her."

"No idea," I said and shrugged. "She probably moved overseas. She was the type."

Lindström looked me over. "I'm mostly interested in knowing if you might be willing to share any new information. Now that you don't have to protect your brother anymore."

"There are two months left," I pointed out. "You could still put him away."

He flashed a smile and gave the Bronzol tube a good shake, presumably to get an idea of how many were left.

"On my honor," he said and slipped the tube into his inside breast pocket. "You don't think that these old retiree's hands want to dig something up that's been buried for all these years?" He turned his palms up and looked at them and then at me with an expression of utter innocence. "Anything," he said. "I'm interested in anything at all. It's not impossible that you kept a thing or two to yourselves, you and that friend of yours. You were only fourteen, and it's hard to know what to do in a situation like that." He paused and hid his hands under the table, as if they weren't really living up to his expectations. "And it's possible there was another person at Gennesaret that night."

"Another person?" I asked. "You mean Ewa Kaludis?"

He sighed again.

"No, the fact of the matter is we were never sure if she was there or not. That, too, remains a mystery. She denied it. Henry denied it. It's not necessarily more complicated than that. We could never prove she was with him. But in any case there were indications that Henry had company."

I thought for a few seconds. Mostly about the word "indications."

"Who might that have been?"

"That's what I was hoping you could tell me," said Lindström.

"I haven't the faintest idea," I said. "Might be best to contact Edmund. He was awake for a while that night."

Lindström picked up a handkerchief and blew his nose. "We've already talked," he explained somewhat impatiently. "Twice."

"Did he give you anything?"

"Hmm," said Lindström. "Priests are among the worst subjects of interrogation. Lucky that they're not involved most of the time ... Priests and pimps, I can't tell who I like less."

"All right, then," I said.

We just sat there a moment. Lindström's college-ruled notebook was next to his plate, and as he ceremoniously folded his handkerchief, he kept glancing at its pages, deep in thought. He didn't seem to be any happier for it, or more illuminated. A sense of gloom spread across the table.

"Most unsolved murders have a number of factors in common," he finally said and closed the notebook.

"Really?" I said. "What are they?"

"First and foremost: simplicity," said Lindström. "With Berra Albertsson ... all the murderer had to do was take two steps and whack him with the hammer. Or the sledgehammer or whatever it was. One single blow, and it was done. Bury the murder weapon and forget about the whole story ... Maybe hope for rain during the morning hours, and rain it did."

He fell silent and speared a few stray peas with his fork. He studied them on the tines—as if he'd suddenly realized Berra Albertsson's murderer was hiding inside one of the peas.

Being a detective your whole life must do a number on you, I thought. Another thirty seconds passed.

"How did the murderer know that Albertsson was going to be there?" I asked. "It seems odd. I've always wondered."

"There's another possible scenario," said Lindström. "Berra Albertsson could have been hit by a person who was in the car with him. Someone who might have been in the back seat, for example."

"Why?" I said. "Who would that have been?"

"Good question," Lindström said. "Regardless of who hit him, the motive is problematic."

"If it wasn't Henry?"

"Or Ewa Kaludis," Lindström said.

After giving this some thought, I asked: "How do you know that an unknown person was at Gennesaret that night?"

Lindström hesitated.

"An eye-witness account."

"An eye-witness account? And who the heck provided that?"

"I can't get into it," Lindström said, with an apologetic shrug. "I'm sorry."

Surprised, I took him in for a second. "And the forensic evidence," I asked. "Clues and murder weapons and whatnot, how did that turn out?"

"Poorly," said Lindström. "On all accounts. The rain destroyed all the evidence at the crime scene. We couldn't even tell which of the cars had arrived first, your brother's or Berra's. Even if their positioning suggested that Henry had arrived earlier."

"And the weapon?"

"It was never found," Lindström stated. "No, it is what it is. As long as no one comes forward, Bertil Albertsson's assailant will go free. In two months he'd be free in any case ... but it would be a bonus to be able to write in my memoirs that the case is solved. And anyway I know who did it. That's why I'm sitting here. Hmm."

He paused. Drank the last drop of wine and wiped his mouth. Collected himself before launching his final attack.

"And you don't have anything that might shed some light on the story? Something you held back or only remembered later?"

"No," I said. "I've thought about this for twenty-five years and I know as little today as I knew back then. A madman who committed a random murder, that's where I'd put my money. Have you really exhausted that possibility?"

Lindström didn't answer.

"Of course I would have turned to the police if I'd known anything," I added.

By now Lindström was starting to look resigned. I didn't have much left of the respect I'd felt for him in the early sixties. A fourteen-year-old probably isn't a great judge of character, even if my brother had complimented me about exactly this.

"I'm sorry," I said. "I'm very sorry, but it looks like this trip of yours to Gothenburg won't be much of a success."

"Don't say that," said Lindström. "The food could have been worse and I've got another conversation on the schedule."

"Oh?" I said. "With whom?"

He adjusted the Bronzol tube in his breast pocket and looked out the window.

I never worked out if Verner Lindström really did have another subject to interview during his Gothenburg trip, but two months later the Bertil Albertsson case was statute-barred. It was September 1987, and only afterward did Ewa and I realize that on the night the statute of limitations ran out, we'd happened to have shared a lobster and a bottle of champagne.

As if we'd known about the date and deemed it worthy of celebration, somehow.

The real reason was that Karla had gone to visit her dad in Eslöv and for once we had the apartment on Palmstedtsgatan to ourselves.

24

The years passed and things slipped into oblivion. Ewa Kaludis and I never had any children: we'd run out of time. She was forty-seven when we reunited, and both of us thought it was too risky. Her daughter Karla lived with us until about 1990, when she went off to study something or other in Paris, met a dark, wavy-haired Frenchman, and stayed. The frequency of my own children's visits increased at about the same rate as Ellinor's ire dissipated, and my eldest son, Frans, lived with us for a few months one autumn during his first semester studying journalism.

Even though Ewa's periods stopped a few months after she turned fifty, our love life didn't go through any corresponding changes. As far as I could tell, from discreet conversations I had with colleagues and others, we had an unusually robust sex life. No one could ever guess that there were ten years between us; I often have a hard time getting my head around it myself.

I guess that's how it is. Time leaves no mark on some, and on others you can count the years double or triple.

The final chapter in the history of Gennesaret—or the Incident, as I liked to call it once upon a time—was written during the spring and summer of 1997.

One day in early May, my ex-wife, Ellinor, informed me that Father Wester up in Ånge had suffered a heart attack and was hospitalized in Östersund. He was most likely on his deathbed, and because he still had Ellinor's phone number from the visit twelve years prior, he'd called her asking to speak with me.

Of course I wasn't surprised to hear about Edmund's heart attack, considering his enormous body, and I decided to travel up to Östersund as soon as possible.

The opportunity arose a few days later, on Ascension Day, and I had four days off. I considered my travel options—plane, train, or automobile—and settled on taking the car. I set off early on Thursday morning and about ten hours later I took my place in a tubular steel chair by Edmund's side.

He hadn't got any smaller since our last meeting; he lay beneath a yellow blanket like a stranded walrus, and a considerable number of tubes were stuck into his arms and legs, pumping nourishment through his tremendous body. His face was grayish purple, like a moldy plum, and it was hard to tell if he'd pull through.

Whatever the case, he seemed relieved to see me.

"So, tell me: how did things go with your father?" I said. "Your real one. Did you ever look him up?"

Edmund gave a quick, strained smile.

"Yes, I looked him up," he said. "He was in a home outside Lycksele. Didn't recognize me. I don't think he remembered that he had a son—alcoholism and mismanaged diabetes. He died a few months after."

I nodded. Of course that's how it would go. It was typical, somehow. Edmund seemed reluctant to talk about it; he had neither the desire nor the energy. There was a more pressing matter to attend to before it was too late.

A little over half an hour into our conversation, he grew too weak to continue. When we were done Edmund looked as peaceful as only the dead and severely ailing can. One of the last things he said was:

"It was still one helluva summer, Erik. In spite of the Incident, it was one helluva summer. I'll never forget it."

"Neither will I," I promised and patted him between two of the needles. "Not for as long as I live."

"Not for as long as I live," Edmund repeated matter-of-factly.

And then he fell asleep. I stayed a while and watched him, and suddenly I became aware that he was no longer in the hospital bed, but floating on his back in the lake at Gennesaret that sultry night after watching the pageantry of love through the window.

And I wished dearly for him to remain there.

I left with a sense of closure. Checked out of Hotel Zäta and headed south again. During the drive through the forests in Dalarna and Värmland, I decided to commit this whole story to paper. Write it down and try to get it the right way around. If what I read somewhere is true—that every person has a book inside of them—then mine would be the story of the murder of Berra Albertsson.

But it wasn't mine alone.

I started on it as soon as we broke up for summer vacation, and at the end of June—the week after Midsummer—I took a research trip back to the landscape of my childhood. Ewa hummed and hawed for a long time about whether or not to join me, but in the end she decided to stay at home, because Karla had spontaneously and gleefully announced that she was thinking of coming for a visit with her Frenchman.

I hadn't set foot in the town on the plain since we'd moved away in the early sixties, and when the beautiful jasmine-scented summer night came rolling into my car as I drove along Stenevägen, I felt myself sinking down into the well of time.

So much had changed, but even more was just the same as ever. The exterior of the house on Idrottsgatan had been renovated, but the colors were the same and in the kitchen window facing the street were two pelargoniums, just like there used to be. I parked the car, walked out through the stretch of woodland and found the cement pipe in the ditch.

No one had touched it for thirty-five years. I had to crouch to fit, but never mind; I lit a cigarette, a Lucky Strike I'd bought at the railway station kiosk in Hallsberg. I shut my eyes and sat inside, smiling and close to tears.

What is a life? I thought. What is a goddamn life?

I thought about Benny and Benny's mom; about Enok and Balthazar Lindblom and Edmund.

About my mother and father.

And Henry.

About the day a thousand years ago that Ewa Kaludis came riding into Stava School on her red Puch. Kim Novak.

And about my father's words: *We're looking at a rough summer, boy. Let's face it.*

My mother's limp hair and dying eyes in the hospital. What is a life?

The pattern of tiles in the bathroom. The tiny scars on Edmund's feet, proof he'd once had twelve toes.

Ewa Kaludis. Her warm, strong hands on my shoulders, and her naked body.

She's all I have left.

All I have managed to keep, I thought, is Ewa's beautiful body.

It could have been worse.

On the way out of town, I took Mossbanegatan south. Karlesson's shop was where it always was, although the gum dispenser was no longer there. However, the business had been extended as a corner cafe; it was called Gullan's Grill now and I didn't feel like stopping.

The Kleva hill was as steep as ever, even if it was less noticeable sitting in the comfort of the car. I could still identify the place where Edmund had lain down and vomited after his valiant effort to conquer it all in one go, and the road through the forest to Åsbro was the same down to every last bend. In the village itself they'd added a gas station, but overall it was as I remembered it. I stopped outside Laxman's. I went in and bought a Ramlösa and an evening paper. The heavy-set woman at the till was in her fifties and had blooms of sweat under her arms, and there was nothing that spoke against her being Britt Laxman.

A number of new summer houses had been built along Sjölyckevägen, but when I reentered the forest I still knew every twist and dip of the winding gravel path. The Levis' house looked boarded up, but it had back then, too. I remembered the incantation as I drove past. Cancer-Treblinka-Love-Fuck-Death. I thought of Edmund's real dad sitting at the edge of his bed and crying for himself and for his abused boy, and then the memories came flooding back, and I didn't realize I'd arrived at the parking area until I was standing on it.

The clearing seemed to have shrunk. Weeds and brushwood had encroached on its edges; maybe this was temporary but it seemed to be disused. I climbed out of the car and took in the start of both paths: the left down to the Lundins' was nearly overgrown; the right to Gennesaret looked trodden on and used. After a moment's hesitation I followed it down to the lake.

Gennesaret was where it had been, too. The same warped little hovel, but repainted and with a new roof. A garden shed out on the lawn and white garden furniture instead of our old rickety brown set. An outdoor grill and a TV antenna.

Nineties versus sixties. Forty-nine instead of fourteen.

Both the door and the kitchen window were open, so I knew there was someone home. I didn't want to have to explain my errand, so I stayed on the path. Looked at everything through a lens thirty-five years thick; both the outhouse and the old shed were still there, and—above all—the pontoon dock. I was startled by my lingering pride and before the tears started to fall, I turned on my heels and went right back up the path to the parking spot.

I took the spade out of the trunk of the car, walked straight across the road, measured between the trees, and had no trouble finding the small mossy hollow.

I drove the spade into the earth and dug out a few shovels' worth. By the third dig, I hit the shaft. I wedged the blade underneath and soon I was standing there with the sledgehammer in my hands.

It was lighter than I'd remembered, but less ravaged by time than anything else I'd seen that day. Otherwise it was exactly as I recalled. I gingerly brushed the shaft and the head clean. When the earth and muck were gone, it could just as well have been lying among the other tools in the shed all this time. It could even have been manufactured as recently as a few years ago.

That is to say: If not for a brownish-black, dried-up blotch on one end of the sledgehammer's head. It's incredible how some things endure. Sink their teeth in and endure.

I shunted the mounds of earth back into the hole and covered them with moss. Stuffed the sledgehammer in a black plastic bag. Tossed it into the footwell of the car on the passenger's side and drove away.

Two hours later I watched the bag sink to the bottom of a dark and muddy lake in the woods of Skara. The sun had started to set and the midges buzzed around my head, but I stood there a long while, eyes fixed on the place where the sledgehammer had broken through the water's surface. When there was no trace of it left, I shrugged and started the journey back home to Gothenburg.

A few days later Ewa and I were awake one night after making love. The window was propped wide open; it was one of those rare summer nights that only comes two or three times a year in Sweden. Music and laughter were spilling in from some sort of garden party the neighbors were having.

"That book you're writing?" Ewa asked, caressing my stomach. "How's it going?"

"Well enough," I answered. "It's coming along."

After laying like that a while, she said: "I've always wondered something."

"Oh?" I said. "What?"

"Who actually killed Berra? You or Edmund? It had to be one of you."

I turned around and buried my face between her breasts.

"Truer words were never spoken," I said. "It had to have been one of us."

And then I told her who.

"What?" said Ewa. "I can't hear what you're saying when you speak straight into my body like that."

I breathed in her scent and then that cloud unfurled inside me. Funny how some clouds linger.

SASKIA VOGEL was born and raised in Los Angeles and now lives in its sister city, Berlin, where she works as a writer and Swedish-to-English literary translator. Her translations include *All Monsters Must Die: An Excursion to North Korea* by Magnus Bärtås and Fredrik Ekman, *Who Cooked Adam Smith's Dinner?* by Katrine Marçal, and works of fiction by Rut Hillarp and Lina Wolff, among others. She has recently published her first novel.

On the Design

As book design is an integral part of the reading experience, we would like to acknowledge the work of those who shaped the form in which the story is housed.

Tessa van der Waals (Netherlands) is responsible for the cover design, cover typography, and art direction of all World Editions books. She works in the internationally renowned tradition of Dutch Design. Her bright and powerful visual aesthetic maintains a harmony between image and typography and captures the unique atmosphere of each book. She works closely with internationally celebrated photographers, artists, and letter designers. Her work has frequently been awarded prizes for Best Dutch Book Design.

The cover photograph was taken by Carl Brandt, a copywriter and graphic designer based in Germany, who also has a passion for film and photography. In his own words: "During my childhood, my family used to spend the holidays together in Sweden. However, being very young at the time, my own memories of those days are based more on pictures than on real memories. When my first child was born I took parental leave and we went on a trip of a lifetime discovering Sweden in a van and I let my old memories come alive. This shot was taken at a peaceful lake in the middle of Småland. It is symbolic of our trip: in places like this we found the freedom we were looking for."

The cover has been edited by lithographer Bert van der Horst of BFC Graphics (Netherlands).

Suzan Beijer (Netherlands) is responsible for the typography and careful interior book design of all World Editions titles.

The text on the inside covers and the press quotes are set in Circular, designed by Laurenz Brunner (Switzerland) and published by Swiss type foundry Lineto.

All World Editions books are set in the typeface Dolly, specifically designed for book typography. Dolly creates a warm page image perfect for an enjoyable reading experience. This typeface is designed by Underware, a European collective formed by Bas Jacobs (Netherlands), Akiem Helmling (Germany), and Sami Kortemäki (Finland). Underware are also the creators of the World Editions logo, which meets the design requirement that "a strong shape can always be drawn with a toe in the sand."